THE UMBRA INHERITANCE

Hunter-Mann-Purdy was born in the mid-fifties. As soon as possible (aged 17½) he joined the military where he served for over twenty years. The last six in the Special OP Troop.

He has physically done everything that is written in his books and currently works for corporations, organisations and individuals as a surveillance and courier operative.

He has travelled extensively, and continues to do so.

Published Work:

The Lateo Directive (2007)
Olympia Publishers
ISBN: 978 1905513 21 5

THE UMBRA INHERITANCE

Hunter-Mann-Purdy

THE UMBRA INHERITANCE

Olympia Publishers
London

www.olympiapublishers.com
OLYMPIA PAPERBACK EDITION

Copyright © Hunter-Mann-Purdy 2008

The right of Hunter-Mann-Purdy to be identified as author of
this work has been asserted in accordance with sections 77 and 78 of
the Copyright, Designs and Patents Act 1988.

All Rights Reserved

No reproduction, copy or transmission of this publication
may be made without written permission.
No paragraph of this publication may be reproduced,
copied or transmitted save with the written permission of the publisher,
or in accordance with the provisions
of the Copyright Act 1956 (as amended).

Any person who does any unauthorized act in relation to
this publication may be liable to criminal
prosecution and civil claims for damage.

A CIP catalogue record for this title is
available from the British Library.

ISBN: 978-1-905513-36-9

This is a work of fiction.
Names, characters, places and incidents originate from the writers
imagination. Any resemblance to actual persons, living or dead, is
purely coincidental.

First Published in 2008

**Olympia Publishers
60 Cannon Street
London
EC4N 6NP**

Printed in Great Britain

Dedicated to the men of the Special OP Troup.
That last Endurance Run is a bastard isn't it.

And
To my good friend Big Mac,
who has helped in more ways than one.

Finally
Becky, without whom
none of this would have been possible.
All my love… Mac

Umbra is latin for shadow.

Acknowledgements

Paranoid by Tommi/Butler/Ward/Osbourne

Truly by Lionel Richie

prologue

It is a popular misconception that 'The Hague' is a building; it is not.

Another popular misconception is that Amsterdam has always been the capital of Holland; this is not so.

Admittedly, to its tourist population of weed smoking weekenders it might feel like the greatest city in Holland, maybe even the whole universe; it isn't.

The old capital of South Holland is a city called The Hague, founded around 1500 by a monarchy that still rules today. You might be led to believe, by its laid back attitude, that Holland is one of the most stable countries in the world. And, while that may hold true today, it is a fact that Holland has had more coups d'état and military takeovers than any other country, ever. And yes, that includes the African nations.

It is more famous these days not for its wonderful architecture or its legalised brothels but for the worldwide media coverage given to its International War Crimes Tribunals.

The Hague has hosted many such tribunals, most notably those of Milan Babic and Milomir Stakic, the man responsible for the notorious Prijedor detention camps where an estimated 200,000 men, women and children were brutally, premeditatedly and systematically murdered.

The large grey metal door swung noiselessly open on well-oiled hinges. The guard was unprepared for what he saw but did not let the surprise register on his face.

It was a large room with a high ceiling, similar in dimensions to a Georgian drawing room, with heavy deep coving. The walls were a neutral cream with unidentifiable stains here and there. At one end was a double bed, unmade, a plain chest of drawers, wardrobe and dark carpeting. Another door, half-opened, led to a bathroom with a chipped toilet and cheap plastic seat. The only other item of furniture was a grey steel desk at which the room's only occupant sat. He was a large squat man with straggly white hair, usually neat, now long and unkempt about his ears. The man wore dark grey trousers, an off-white shirt, dirty around the collar, and a V-neck jersey, the type often given by a homely Grandma as an un-thoughtful, hastily wrapped birthday present.

He sat with his back to the guard, writing deliberately as though having difficulty with the words.

He's been here since 2002 but hasn't done much with the place.

"Hmph. Your food sir," said the guard, trying to ensure the man wasn't startled by his unannounced presence.

The man seemed not to hear, then carefully and with great deliberation placed his pen and reading glasses down on the desk.

"Here please corporal," he replied tiredly, in heavily accented English.

The guard placed the plastic tray on the desk as instructed. The man closed his eyes and rubbed the bridge of his nose. After placing the tray the guard stood to the left of the desk and waited.

Opening his eyes, the man studied the meal before him. As usual all the accoutrements – beaker, plates and utensils – were plastic, in an attempt to dissuade him from harming himself with them.

"Whenever I open my eyes it never seems that what I wish for is there." The words were unhurried, the voice wistful.

"And what would you wish for sir?" responded the uniformed man, his voice neutral and even.

The man turned his bull-neck slowly and appraised the guard with eyes that had seen more than anyone was ever meant to.

"You're new here."

"Yes sir." The guard stood at ease, hands behind his back in a deliberate, non-threatening manner.

"I would wish for anything but chicken." The man prodded the boiled boneless meat. "I love chicken. But not four times a week for the last four years."

Taking hold of the beaker he gulped down half the orange-flavoured contents.

"The guards have instructions not to talk to me or anyone else here; why are you?" he asked, replacing the beaker.

"That is because I'm not a guard, sir." he said flatly.

The man froze, then slowly placed the fork on his plate. Staring hard at the warm meal going cold, he took a moment to fully comprehend the meaning of what had just been said. This was the moment for which he had been waiting, expecting, for many years. The realisation struck home; he found it somehow comforting that all this absurdity could now end.

"Finally," he said to himself quietly, his shoulders relaxing at the thought.

"How will you do it? A gun? Too loud. A knife? They may have found it on the entry search. Maybe you are a master of Ninjutsu?" He laughed at himself as relief and adrenaline entered his bloodstream. "So," he stood and walked over to the bed, "what's it to be?"

The man accepted his fate – welcomed it even. He had done terrible things during his life. Sooner or later he knew fate would catch up.

"Do you remember 1998, a village called Trstenik?"

"No, what of it?" he asked, puzzled.

"In that village, men under your command were holding journalists and several female relief aid workers hostage. Under your instructions the females were raped, then killed, then you had the journalists shot also."

"Maybe. It was a long time ago, I don't remember." He waved his hands as though swatting imaginary flies, he didn't want to recall.

"Among the females," he added in the same flat emotionless voice, "and journalists were six British citizens. For their deaths you must now pay."

The man lay back on the bed suddenly weak. He closed his eyes remembering for an instant those terrible surreal days. He remembered Trstenik, all too well.

"So, you're going to kill me?" he asked softly.

"No sir," the guard said conversationally, "...I already have."

The guard closed and locked the cell door, having placed the body in a sleeping position, partially covering it with sheets. As he walked down the corridor he went over the events in his mind, ensuring there were no errors.

He's unconscious now, be dead in under two minutes. The serum I administered via his drink will react with the rifampicin antibiotic he already takes. It will induce a myocardial infarction that'll look like a heart attack in the post-mortem. The doctor from whom I procured the chemicals has no idea what the serum was to be used for, and he's unlikely to see the news. In his Kashmir village they only have one television and that shows non-stop repeats of 'Friends.'

I'll make an anonymous call to the neighbour of the guard whose place I've taken and get him released from his bonds.

Turn right here, up two flights, through the emergency exit. Jump to the next roof over the narrow alley and out onto De Goeff Street.

Even if The Hague security services should get to the bottom of the story, it's unlikely they will want to let the world know how sloppy their security is. They'll go along with the theory that he died of a heart attack induced by mixing medications. If they don't, then they will lose all the subsidies and special allowances that the European Union, via Brussels, bestows. They won't like that.

If he'd still been at the Scheveningen Detention Centre, I'd have had a much harder time getting to him.

I've got fifty minutes before someone collects the tray, maybe longer if they think he's sleeping it off.

Near the boiler in the second building is a suitcase with a change of clothes and passport. I'll be at the train station within thirty minutes, on the 13:00 train to Paris.

Now changed into navy-blue pinstripe suit, black suede shoes, blue-gold tie and white shirt, pork-pie hat and black-framed glasses and was pulling a small grey wheelie Samsonite suitcase, inside which was the guard's uniform.

He hailed a taxi, looking over his shoulder at The Hague Tribunal building.

Justice has been a long time coming, but we got you in the end, Slobodan Milosevic.

chapter one

Lady Philipa Parker-Wainwright sat reflecting in her titanium Range Rover Discovery 4x4. She was happy with her life, she realised. She had reached a high rung in her clothing design business and next week her personal collection of female wear was to be launched. She grinned at the thought, a warm vibrant smile. Her husband had called earlier from New York to say he'd been awarded the contract for a large city development in uptown Manhattan. She never realised just how smutty her husband could be on the phone and caught her reflection in the inside mirror, grinning like a village idiot at the recollection.

During twelve years of marriage they had produced Colombo, their son, for whom she now waited. They'd moved to Kensington eight years ago specifically so that Colombo came within the catchment area of St Luke's School. This school had the highest percentage of university candidates in the United Kingdom and they wanted to give their son every opportunity and advantage they possibly could. Lady Wainwright gripped the leather steering wheel.

Yes, life hasn't been this good since... I don't know when!

She waved energetically through the open window as Colombo appeared at the school gates. All black blazer, thick mop of brown curly hair and a smile to make Brad Pitt jealous.

He's going to break a lot of hearts, mine included, I suspect.

Colombo ran in that out-of-kilter gangly style only children, baby ostriches and Bambi could manage. He opened the front passenger door, climbed in and gave his mum a big, sloppy loving kiss on the cheek, throwing his school bag onto the back seat and slamming the door solidly behind him.

"Good day was it?" she asked, checking the mirror, selecting drive on the automatic gearbox and pulling out into the busy road.

"Fantastic," he enthused, gesticulating excitedly.

"Seat belt, darling."

"Oh yeah, sorry Mummy." He pulled at the belt and fastened it quickly with a metallic snap. "Well… we got this frog yeah, then we made it sleep with chlorowatsits, then…"

"Are you sure I should hear this?" she teased.

Colombo's eyebrows knitted together as he gave serious consideration to her playful jest.

"What do you…"

KABOOOOM !!!

The Discovery weighed two tons and had been designed to withstand heavy impacts, but not from the inside.

Under Lady Wainwright's seat the four-kilo charge of RDX explosive ignited. With its heavy and solid construction the blast was momentarily contained, disintegrating the 4x4 and its occupants. Inertia kept the vehicle moving until it hit a garden wall then stopped. Shards of metal and the concussive wave shattered windows of houses for 150 metres. Colombo's blood-stained school bag was found hanging from a tree two streets away.

chapter two

John McBride laughed uproariously at the on-screen antics. Whenever there was a free moment he would put on an episode of Ultimate Force featuring Ross Kemp from Eastenders and more recently from 'Ross Kemp on Gangs.'

After serving a term of over twenty-years in the British Army, beginning in 1973, he felt he was not only qualified but justified in his viewpoint on the TV series. He especially liked the episode from series four where a group of Russian psychopaths strip to their skin in freezing conditions to show how tough they are while guarding a container of radioactive material on an open rooftop. A detonator is pushed firmly into a block of plastic explosives by about quarter of an inch by one of the Russians.

Firstly, if you push an electric detonator into plastic explosives as hard as that without having first made a tunnel for it with a pencil or biro, it's likely to explode. Second, if you don't push the detonator at least two-thirds of its length into the explosive material, you won't initiate the charge and you're wasting your time.

John found it extremely amusing, hysterically so at times and had christened the show 'Ultimate Farce.' He found it very amusing that no matter where Red Troop of Ultimate Force were supposed to be in the world, it was always Aldershot or Salisbury Plain Training Area.

He'd been addicted to the series from the first episode shown on TV, buying the DVD as soon as it became available. He knew all of the characters by name and would spend whatever free time he had on internet chat-rooms discussing them and their techniques. It was only after series two had been aired that John

25

was told, via the chat-room that Ultimate Force was supposed to be a realistic action series. He was confused for a while as he'd always assumed it was a comedy. This realisation did not deter him from watching his obsession. It just made it funnier.

John had made it to the dizzy heights of sergeant in the elite Pathfinder unit of the Parachute Regiment. Selected only from within the parachute corps, these volunteers underwent a further gruelling selection and training process to equip them with the necessary skills to operate behind enemy lines. The job of the Pathfinders is to be the first men on the ground, clearing pockets of resistance and preparing Landing Zones for the much greater force to follow.

John was a Squad Leader and contrary to the norm invariably took point as Lead Scout on any patrol. Carrying a 'Patchett,' its military designation was L34A1, an almost silent version of the nine-millimetre Sterling sub-machine gun and named after its inventor G.W Patchett. It was John's job to lead the patrol through enemy positions and around obstacles such as minefields, sometimes vice-versa. He was respected by his squad members but not particularly well liked. John wasn't a 'joiner,' he was essentially a loner who worked with but was not part of a team.

He'd been one of the first British soldiers to land on the Falkland Islands during the Argentinean occupation in 1982. His job on that occasion was to clear the summits of several mountain tops that housed Argy observation posts and had troops patrolling in preparation for the coming landings. He was to plot the positions and send the co-ordinates back via frequency hopping burst-transmission radios. Just before the British landings took place the Royal Navy would bombard the locations with their long-range guns and deny the Argy's the ability to see what was going on and more importantly; where.

There was a story going around the Pathfinder unit that John, leading his squad to a Lay-Up-Point before dawn; unexpectedly came across an eight-man Argy patrol. These guys were conscripts admittedly but they had an experienced sergeant-major leading them and they were all carrying 7.62 FN full-auto assault rifles with the safeties off and their fingers on the triggers.

John was twenty-five metres ahead of his team when they heard the dull thud of the silenced Patchett on the crisp night air. Running forward and forming an extended line ready to lay down a devastating volley of fire in support of their commander. They were surprised to see the Argentinean patrol dead where they fell, each with a hole in their forehead. They'd never even seen John as he'd moved through their ranks like an invisible scythe, not one of them had managed to fire off a round.

Of course this is only a rumour but from that night on both his unit and Regiment referred to him as 'Wraith.'

•••

The Intercontinental Phoenicia was a testament to Beiruti durability. Ninety-nine percent of the windows and internal glass had been shattered during the explosion of the February 2005 Harari assassination. Now, in late November of the same year the hotel was not only fully functional but superb. Its decor, service and food were remarkable by any country's standards. In fact, many European and western countries could not compete at this level.

Mac sat in the mosaic restaurant on the ground floor, having passed through a security check and a metal detector in the hotel lobby. The Spectre lock-knife Mac habitually carried had set off the detection machine but security were not concerned with a lock-knife, they were interested only in explosives or automatic weapons. A lock-knife was the least one would be expected to carry on the streets of Beirut; he was waved through without concern.

The restaurant held a mixed bag of guests. Wealthy Lebanese families with overdressed wives and hair firmly in the style of Jackie Onassis. Sri Lanken nannies to look after their over-boisterous spoilt children and elderly couples hell-bent on getting their money's worth from the huge buffet style spread that covered two floors and half the room.

At the dessert carousel Mac was torn between pear tartlet and crème brûlée; as usual, the crème brûlée won. Savouring the textures of smooth filling and crunchy flame-seared brown sugar topping, Mac considered the possibilities of why he'd been summoned to a meeting here in Beirut. It was the same organisation that had contracted the Prime Minister's death some six months previously. It was either a set-up or work. He believed that if his true identity and purpose as a deep cover operative for 'Action 6' were known it would have been easier to have him go to a more remote location and ambush him there. Here, in such a populated area, that scenario seemed unlikely.

So, it appears there is further work for me. Hmm, wonder what they want doing now?

Mac checked his Breitling Avenger Evolution; the meeting was to be held in the Presidential Suite in twenty minutes. He wasn't overly fond of large watches like the Evolution but they did make excellent distraction devices when thrown in an assailant's face. Additionally, with the latest round of anti-money laundering regulations, it was becoming increasingly difficult to walk through airport customs with £20,000 in a briefcase. With the Breitling on his wrist or one of the new Longine models he could walk through with it on his wrist and sell it at the other end for almost the same amount without having any problems.

Motioning for the bill, Mac paid in US dollars and headed for reception.

"Hi." It was a good job the girl behind the reception desk was wearing sunglasses as Mac smiled such a dazzling smile it would have probably burned out her retinas if she didn't have them on.

"What floor is the Presidential Suite on please?"

The full breasted Lebanese woman smiled back invitingly, just as she did with every male guest, nothing personal you understand.

"We have three Presidential Suites sir, do you have a name?"

"De Sousa, Mr De Sousa." Mac passed on the contact name he'd been given.

The receptionist checked the hotel's database and quickly came up with details.

"Eighth floor, sir." The professional hotelier's smile etched in place, her bosom threatening to dislodge the computer screen from the desk top. The elderly man to Mac's right almost walked into a display cabinet, his fixation with the assistant's breasts attracting his attention like a moth to a flame.

"Thank you," replied Mac as he headed for the cedar-panelled elevators to the right of the reception desk, neatly sidestepping the elderly moth.

Mac ran his hand over the smooth wooden surface, the natural scent from which filled his nostrils with a heady musk.

I wonder if these panels are from the famous Cedars of Lebanon? The musk repels unwanted insects; maybe that's why they use them?

The doors swished open and ended Mac's pondering. He exited and walked down the long brightly lit corridor adorned with classic Greek-style pictures in gold frames.

The large dark-stained wooden door had a brass plaque affixed; the words "Presidential" emblazoned across its surfaced. Mac knocked.

With a whoosh of air the door was jerked swiftly open; a large evenly tanned man took a step back and bade Mac enter. There were two of them.

Dick and Dom.

Dick closed the door then patted Mac down for weapons as Dom looked down and tried to make eye contact. Mac only came up to Dom's chest so not making eye contact wasn't a problem. They were in a small reception area made smaller by the huge bulk of the bodyguards.

Dick grunted as he found the hard metal edge of the Spectre in Mac's waistband. Handing it over, Mac made it clear he'd be wanting it back when he left; the only response that he heard was a second non-committal grunt.

Having ensured Mac wasn't carrying any additional weaponry, Dick and Dom took a step back in unison and indicated that Mac should go to the right, around the partition wall. As Mac entered the main living area he took in the surroundings; mustard curtains, light beige carpet, oval black marble coffee table, standard 42 inch wall-mounted plasma screen, low ceiling. In the arched recesses old table urns had been turned into lamps; Mac couldn't help but feel let down by the decor.

As the seated man raised himself from the dark leather chair he launched his hand firmly forward.

"My friend, my very good friend," said the tall thin middle-eastern gentleman, who was dressed in an expensive dark apple suit and cream coloured open-necked shirt. Mac noticed the Paget watch inlaid with diamonds. The man was around six feet two, bald with just a hint of black hair at his temples; cadaverous – he looked in need of a good meal.

If it wasn't for the tan and tash he'd be a dead ringer for Norman Tebbit.

Mac couldn't take his eyes off the incongruous deep black moustache; it seemed to have a life of its own, slug-like.

Mac extended his hand which was shaken vigorously and with obvious sincerity.

Maybe a little too much sincerity.

"I have been looking forward to this meeting for many weeks, please sit, sit."

The man didn't introduce himself, and Mac didn't ask.

"May I get you some refreshment?"

"No, thank you," Mac replied, looking around the room. Through open doors on the far side he could make out a bedroom and an office of sorts.

Once Mac sat in the offered chair, Dick and Dom stood behind to his left and right, too close as far as Mac was concerned.

"I am assured that you are a man of great competence. A man who can disappear and re-appear at will. A man who can achieve the impossible. A man..." Mac raised his hand, Skinny abruptly stopped the rehearsed compliments.

"I am here to be briefed for work, is that correct?"

Norman nodded, unsure.

"Then these two," Mac waved his hand in the direction of Dick and Dom, "need to be somewhere else."

Norman understood: these men need not know the details of this meeting. This man was truly as impressive as he had been led to believe, a paradox, considering how ordinary he at first appeared. At five foot six the man was of average height, slim build, short grey hair – virtually an average, instantly forgettable guy.

This man is spoken of with great esteem and not a little fear. But he is right, this is a matter between men of power and not for the ears of the hired help.

Norm said something quick and unintelligible to the bookends and they turned to leave. Mac stood quickly and held out his hand to the departing figures. Dick, on some Neanderthal level understood and looked toward Norm who curtly nodded assent. Taking out the knife, Dick handed over the Spectre to the waiting palm. Dick was by no means an innocent, he'd been involved in many turf wars in the back streets of Syria. A one time jailer and interrogator, he was no stranger to physical violence nor inflicting pain on others; he welcomed confrontation in whatever form. He would very much like to crush this arrogant little man with the hand held open.

Dick finally made eye contact and was completely taken aback by what he saw; the grey-green eyes normally full of intelligence and humour, now filled with desolation, emptiness; the cold, cold eyes chilled him to the marrow. He felt the chill, like an ice-pick entering his heart. As he handed over the Spectre he couldn't help himself.

"Sorry," he said quietly.

Mac smiled; it wasn't pretty.

chapter three

Angus McDougal was a keen, albeit amateur, outdoorsman. His estate of almost five-hundred acres was a few miles north-west of Kirkcaldy, Fife and had been in the family for over four centuries. The estate was a constant drain on his resources and Angus was perpetually concerned by the financial crises that loomed. He didn't want to be the last of the McDougals, nor did he want to be the one responsible for the estate's demise. Unless he came up with a startling plan of action soon it could be the first step down a very slippy financial slope. He had been offered a lifeline by a property developer keen to purchase fifty acres of grazing land at the far end of the estate. Angus had two more days to decide if he wanted to sell. He already knew the answer; of course he didn't want to sell but he had to and that was a different thing entirely. It was a constant source of irony and amusement to Angus that in his professional capacity he was considered a financial wizard. A man who rescued other companies and individuals from the brink of bankruptcy.

If only I could rescue myself!

Angus arrived home after a long day of meetings and mergers in Edinburgh, eager to spend the evening out in the woodlands with Casey, an alpha-male retriever. Eager too, to put all the financial problems behind him, even if it was only temporarily, he parked the S-type Jaguar on the mile-long gravel drive; it had barely stopped before he leapt out, guilty with anticipation, knowing he should spend some time with his wife and spoilt children.

Later, he said to himself indulgently.

Casey met Angus excitedly in the hallway, tail wagging vigorously. Angus petted Casey lest he bark and alert the family waiting in the east-wing. He quickly made his way to the study and locked gun cabinet. Taking the key from his waistcoat pocket, he turned it and hefted the Purdey shotgun, his favourite. Grabbing a bandolier of twelve-gauge shells, hat and Wellingtons, Angus headed off down the track, the woodlands not too far off in the distance.

Just for an hour or so.

The gun was beautifully balanced; Angus rubbed his hands appreciatively over the oiled surface. Casey trotting along beside, tongue hanging out, panted happily.

Angus had only just made it into the woodline when he began to feel uncomfortably warm. Taking off his deerstalker hat, he paused as his breathing became difficult, laboured.

"Well Casey, I must be much more out of condition than I thought or maybe those oysters at lunch were a bit off, eh?"

Angus reached down to ruffle Casey's neck fur but somehow ended up on the fern-laden floor. The air rattled in his throat, his eyelids twitched uncontrollably; froth foamed at lips contorted with pain. His body convulsing, his spine arched with every spasm. Twenty seconds later he was dead.

Casey nudged at his fallen master, whined, then sat. He would wait patiently until the body was found, two days later.

Ricin, a poisonous substance derived from Mexican beans had been added to the gun oil that had liberally coated the shotgun. Absorbed through the skin and exacerbated by exercise, it had stopped Angus's heart in under ten minutes.

chapter four

Having joined as a Junior Para at the age of sixteen, John McBride had two long years of brutalisation at the hands of the Permanent Training Cadre. He'd made it through the gruelling selection and training process and graduated to adult military service at the age of eighteen. He was immediately shipped out to join 3 Para on a tour of South Armagh in Northern Ireland.

During that tour John realised why the Training Staff had been so harsh in their treatment of the Junior Paras. They were preparing them for war as best they could. War that was to leave an indelible mark on one particular soldier...John McBride.

John made a lot of mistakes during that four-month tour but there always seemed to be an 'old sweat' around, an old sweat was considered to be someone who'd served ten-years or more. First they would take-the-piss then, show him how it should be done. By the last few weeks of the tour, John was hooked. He ate slept and breathed army. During any 'sack time' when he should have been resting he could be found sat in one of the corrugated tin and concrete sangers, reading military handbooks, survival magazines or some other how-to-book that he'd purchased through Paladin or Delta Press, both American book companies that specialised in unusual literature. If you wanted to pick a lock, build an atomic bomb or get revenge on your boss, Paladin Press had a book for each occasion.

The first fifteen-years flew by, John loved every minute of it but felt there was also something lacking in his own personal life. It was about this time that he met and married Gracie, a local Aldershot girl who worked in the NAAFI, which was a cafe-come-meeting place where everyone congregated in the evenings to drink beer, tell lies and fight each other.

Ten-months later Rachael was born and John finally felt complete. This was what he had been missing but never fully comprehended until he held her in his arms. His happiness lasted five-months at which time his beloved Gracie was killed by a driver high on amphetamines. John was given time to grieve and arrange a nanny for Rachael. He knew the other option was a compassionate discharge but that would resolve nothing.

His parents were willing but were simply too old to cope with a small child but with the insurance money from Gracie's death John could afford a full-time live-in nanny from a reputable agency.

Over the next few years John was away from home for nearly ten-months of every year and saw little of Rachael who adored her father somewhat unreasonably, as children often do.

Two-years short of a full twenty-two years service John became unhappy with the time spent away from his daughter and applied for voluntary redundancy. After a wait of four-months he received a letter informing him that his application had been successful and left the service with a golden handshake of £56,000 and an index linked pension of almost £300 per month. He took Rachael back to his home town of Manchester and settled in a Council property arranged for him by the army's resettlement board. He ended up living not three streets away from where he'd been born.

It didn't take long for John to realise that his recollections of the place he used to live were somewhat rose-tinted. The friendliness and solidarity of the people in the area had vanished, replaced with drugs, alcohol fuelled aggression and ASBOs. Rachael was nearly six and John had spent less than a year and a half with his daughter. He determined he would at least try to make it up to her.

Rachael went to the local school where she could mix with non-military children. John would walk her to school and at the end of lessons would be at the gates waiting to walk her home. Rachael didn't mind, in fact, she thought it was cute in a Sir Galahad sort of way. Cute was not a word often used by members of the Pathfinders when describing the Wraith.

John was trying really hard to fit in with his new lifestyle but it wasn't easy. Rising at 6am he would run five miles as fast as he could, feel the burn in his lungs, taste the blood at the back of his throat, and feel what it was like to be alive. He would return in time to make Rachael breakfast then get her ready for school. After dropping her off he would get back to the house, tidy and clean. Finishing in time for his 10.30 NAAFI break of coffee and a bacon roll from the local cafe. He'd struck up an acquaintanceship with Peggy, a thirty-something blond with a husband who disappeared six-months ago and two children of Rachael's age. When John came into the cafe everyone noticed the harsh lines vanish from her face and her usual brusque manner soften, everyone but John.

Around lunchtime John would stroll around the once pretty; graffiti and rubbish strewn estate. Young teenagers, who should be at school, wandered the streets intent on impressing scantily clad girls of a similar age. Alcoholic 'fruit' drinks; a foul mouth and cigarettes their staple diet.

"Hey mate. Wanna buy some gear?" asked a hooded youth, his face pock-marked and oily, hair lank and unkempt, eyes darting from side-to-side in apprehension. In John's world the word 'gear' meant equipment, web belts, knives and ammunition, he was momentarily confused as to why someone would sell such items on a street corner.

"What kind of gear?" he asked curiously.

"I got Moroccan, Skunk, uppers, downers, ecstasy and if you want sumfin I aint got, I can get it, ya get me?" the young boy smiled with brown stained teeth and swollen gums. John could see the hollowness of his cheeks, eyes darkened by ill health and burst blood vessels. He was aghast, which quickly turned to disgust. He shook his head and walked briskly away.

"Ya no where to come, yeh?" shouted the pusher intent on ensuring a sale at some point. John was still fuming as he turned the corner to the street his house was on. His mind whirling as he remembered his wife's death and the driver high on drugs. With his focus on painful memories he almost bumped into the group of boys sat on his garden wall passing a joint from one to the other.

"Get the fuck off my wall," rasped John through gritted teeth; in no mood for small talk.

"Your wall? Your wall? Don't you get it old man? Dis is our wall yeh. We just let you use it," he grinned, showing a diamond set in yellow teeth. He nodded to his mates as if looking for corroboration, they jeered.

John realised that his first outburst wasn't the way to handle this group and raised his hands in appeasement.

"Now look kids. I don't want any trouble but I don't want you sitting on my wall and creating a nuisance either ok? So how about you go and hassle somebody else."

Their leader, wearing this weeks must-have Nike trainers, baggy jeans falling around his arse and a grubby Dolce and Gabbana sweat-top hopped down from the waist-high wall and approached John menacingly with his forefinger extended ready to poke him in the chest; punctuating the words already forming in his brain. To this would-be-gangsta John was just a slightly taller than average skinny old man who had too much mouth for his own good. He couldn't let anyone from the estate talk to him like that, others might get the idea that they could do it as well.

Gangsta made half the distance between them before he felt his finger crushed by a vice-like grip; then snapped. He never even saw the man move. Dropping to his knees with the pain of his broken finger, he screamed.

"What you've dun? You'll be sorry." he shouted, getting to his feet, clutching the finger to his chest. "You'll be fuckin' sorry, you're dead; dead. You get me fucker?" Throughout the tirade John stood simply and naturally with his hands by his sides. Gangsta looked behind at his brethren.

"Come on. We've got fings ta do but we'll be back for you fucker, layta yeah," then with as much menace as he could muster took his gang and left the street.

Fuckin punks! A couple of years in the army would sort you out. Those that survived anyway.

John shrugged his shoulders, opened his front door, took off his jacket and went through to what he thought of as the 'front' room. When he was a kid the front room was where all the best furniture and carpets were kept for special visitors. In John's case it was where he kept his books and photographs. He was a keen militarist, his favourite period being the Napoleonic and Crimean campaigns. His library was extensive and the many books, user handbooks and manuals were bang up to date on techniques and equipment as well as how to load a Brown Bess musket whilst under cavalry charge from mounted Chasseurs.

It was nearly two-hours later, as John was firmly engrossed in 'A History of the Spetsnaz,' a factual book on the Russian Special Forces, when the first of three house-bricks came crashing through his windows. John dived, rolled and came up running into the narrow hallway, taking the stairs three at a time and into the bathroom. He stood on the toilet seat and looked through the half-open window as a vantage point hoping to see what exactly was going on outside.

•••

Mac lay still on the king-size bed of the owner's stateroom aboard the 105-foot Sunseeker Manhattan.

The tremendous migraine had hit him just as he made it to the quayside. He'd staggered up the gangplank as the first blinding wave of pain broke across his forehead. This was the way it had been for many years, ever since Iraq. Once Mac received instructions for a mission and he was in a safe haven his brain imploded. For the duration of the intense headache Mac could only lie down, keep still and wait for the atomic explosion in his brain and the waves of nausea to subside. It was never the same twice, sometimes it would be a blinding immobilising flash of pain over twenty minutes. Other times, like now, it lasted for several energy-sapping hours. A solid groaning, searing, knife-like pain. Mac knew better than to try and move, it only made things worse.

"How long's he been in there?" asked Manny of Andras in a concerned tone.

"Three hours." He looked at his watch. "...nearly."

"Hmph," Manny responded and walking out of the cockpit and onto the rear main deck, lit a cigarette. Manny had accepted Mac's offer of employment five months previously. They'd met in Cyprus at the Limassol docks. Mac had liked the gruff engineer and had persuaded Manny to let him use his boss's boat, taking him to Monaco. Andras had been a security guard at the Limassol marina where the boat had been moored and Manny had employed him as cook and cleaner, as he was family after all.

They were both pleased and excited at captaining a 105-foot Sunseeker although Manny hid his delight very well. It wouldn't do for anyone to see him in anything but his best 'gruff' manner. There were another two crew members hired by Manny, who'd said it would be better for them if they had a vacation from Cyprus for a while. Mac took him at his word that they were good, solid, dependable men who knew how to fight and, more importantly, when to stay quiet. With the money Mac was paying them there would be no complaints from anyone.

The cool evening breeze wafted Manny's smoke out over the stern and it slowly dissipated, creating ethereal shapes in its wake. He looked out over the water at the shimmering moonlit sea. Gulls noiselessly for a change, flew drowsily overhead. His thoughts were calm and peaceful.

"You'll get cancer and die before you reach old age."

Manny turned quickly at the unexpected voice. Mac appeared from the shadows like an ethereal spectre.

"So, it's over?"

"Yeah," said Mac as he pulled the ornate Kimono style dressing gown tight around his body. He'd explained to Manny how the migraine worked.

"A job?"

"Yeah," said Mac flatly.

"Will you need the boat?"

"No, no this time." Mac reconsidered, "take it to Hong Kong, I'll meet you there when I'm done. We've done the Caribbean, let's sail up the coast of China and Shanghai. Maybe we'll stop over in Japan, have a change of scenery."

"Japan? Ok, I'll let Andras know." Manny flicked the cigarette into the sea, walked towards the cockpit, stopped and turned, jerking a thumb upwards.

"He worries about you, you know," meaning Andras, the youngest crewmember.

Mac's pale sweat-glistened face reflected in the early moonlight.

"I know," he answered tiredly.

Manny turned and walked away, grumbling under his breath as he usually did.

Mac stood on the aft sundeck, still weak from the onslaught of the pain. His kimono, predominantly red with a large gold sun silhouetting white cranes, fluttered in the Mediterranean breeze.

The migraine was Mac's defence mechanism for the stress he would be under during the mission. As the pain built up, his brain dissected the information he'd been given, worked out logistics, projected survival percentages, what equipment he'd need and an initial plan of action. He never understood how this happened, he just accepted it did.

Gazing out into the evening sky over the stern of the "Sicilian Princess," Mac spoke to the waves lapping at the descender platform and the cool evening breeze.

"Step one... Becky."

chapter five

Bavaria
12 years earlier

Mac and three other members of the long-range reconnaissance team sat in the Patrol Divisions classroom, listening to a lecture on what foods there are to be had in the wild.

The 'Prussian Palace' or more usually the 'Palace' was a special forces school in Weingarten, Bavaria.

As part of their twenty-six-week selection process members of the Special OP Troop, a deep penetration unit into enemy territory, attended several two-week courses. These included, Resistance to Interrogation, Advanced Specialist Recognition, Close Quarter Fighting, Improvised Weapons and Patrolling Skills. The course they were on at present was Escape and Evasion, the lesson 'Living off the Land.'

It was the fourth day of the course and the previous day everyone had been instructed to bring in a live worm. The tall, rangy, bedraggled and bearded SAS instructor was referred to by his peers as 'Lofty.' He was a dead-ringer for Worzel Gummidge, less the warts.

"You all got yur worms?" asked Lofty in a deep Devon accent.

The class of eighteen students held up their worms as one.

"Right then. I'm gonna heat up this pan 'n throw in a coupla eggs. When I come round I want ya to throw yur worms inta the pan, right."

Lofty pulled out a small single burner calor gas stove; it lit with a roar.

"Now, before we eat the worms, they need ta be strained. As they makes their way through the earth grains of soil pass through the worm from one end ta other. If ya don't strain it yu'll get lots o grit, 'n ya don't want that."

Lofty took a worm he'd brought in and dipped it into a jar of water then, holding the worm by one end, gently squeezed and ran his other fingers down the worm's length. Once he'd done this he held up a tissue on which the extruded grit from the worm had landed.

"See," Lofty said triumphantly, "now, everyone do that."

The class obeyed then, once strained, the worms were added to the eggs.

"A la worm omelette," said chef Lofty. "Right, everyone will 'av a taste." Lofty moved around the class, no-one dared refuse.

It was Mac's turn. Placing a spoonful in his mouth, he chewed. Hmm. He certainly didn't expect it to taste so good.

"Pound for pound there's more protein in a worm than in best steak." Lofty continued.

Pete, one of the team, was looking a little pale and barely tasted the omelette. It wasn't that he was shy or didn't like the idea, he just wasn't feeling too well.

Last night Pete had gone out for a few beers, see what the local girls were up to. After one too many beers he'd decided, as it was nearly midnight, to take a short-cut back to camp via the surrounding fields. Along the way Pete was caught short, and needed to pee. He selected a random bush, unzipped and began to spray his piss in a long arc.

The first anyone knew about it was being woken by screams of "My fuckin' cock! My cock's on fire!!" as he burst into the accommodation, switching the lights on. Pete was inconsolable and was happy to show his dick to anyone who might ease the pain. Mac and the team stripped Pete and put him in a cold shower, which seemed to ease the fiery sensation.

As Pete explained what he'd been doing it became evident what had transpired. In Germany and throughout Europe, cattle were stopped from grazing on too much land at a time by thin wires. These wires were strung up about two-feet off the ground and a high electric current was pulsed through at four to five second intervals. Pete, in the darkness, had pissed on one of these wires and the current had entered his body through his dick, not pleasant at the best of times.

Pete now had to endure several days of ribald jokes and being made fun of. For the remainder of the course the team would wake early, it being a matter of honour to be the first to say, in a loud voice:

"Can anyone else smell bacon?"

chapter six

The mobile phone rang. Only Mac ever called her on that phone.
He's not scheduled to call?
They had been seeing each other every two weeks or so over the last few months. They always stayed on the boat; Becky smiled to herself as she remembered what Mac had named it. They'd been to Trinidad and Tobago, Grenada, Turks and Caicos and another dozen or so Caribbean islands whose names she couldn't recall.

George, her current boyfriend, seemed to accept the relationship she and Mac had – well, if acceptance meant sulking whenever she said she was going away.

Becky pressed the answer button.
"Hi," she said cheerfully.
"Hi, sweetheart, how's the interpreters' course coming along?"
"Ok," Becky replied, not meaning a word of it.
"Do you have a few weeks to spare?"
"Maybe."
"You know the Sunday Times crossword?"
"Yeah."
"Well, question twenty-two, D-eight, the answer is... five days."
Work? ...about time.
"Are you sure that's the answer?" Becky teased.
"If you don't think you can make it, tell me now." Mac's voice became gruff, stern.
"I can make it... no problem," answered Becky demurely, chastised.
"Good... can't wait to see you," said Mac soothingly.

"Me neither." Becky grinned.
"See you soon."
"Yes... Mac?"
"Yes."
"I miss you too."
Becky hung up thinking maybe she'd said too much.
Not like Becky to use my name like that?
"Drat!" said Becky to herself.
I promised myself I wouldn't say anything about missing him... double drat.

As Becky scolded herself she got off the bed, padded over to the bookcase and sifted through the reference books. Pulling down a large world atlas, Becky turned the pages.

Page twenty-two is...
"South Africa?"
D-eight is...
"Durban?"

It really was a good idea of Mac's to have identical atlases. He always means two days less than he says. Better get down to the travel agents and book a flight.

Becky threw on an overcoat, grabbed her black Louis Vuitton bag and flew out of the apartment like a whirlwind.

It was only halfway down the street that she realised she was humming, "Oh happy day..."

•••

The runway at Johannesburg International airport was drying quickly after a violent downpour. Mac alighted the 747-400 and followed signs to baggage claim. Retrieving the grey Samsonite wheelie case he headed to passport control and immigration; from there, taking the *nothing to declare* channel at customs, handed in his customs form. In less than ten minutes from picking up his case Mac was following signs for domestic departures in terminal two.

After re-registering at the ticket desk, he handed over his case once again. Mac wandered the terminal trying to kill the ninety minute wait for the Durban connection.

There wasn't much to see but it amused Mac when he went to the gents toilets and saw a 'Firearms Distribution Point' sign. If travelling within South Africa and some of the other states, you could hand in legally held firearms and collect them at your destination.
Now that's what I call civilised.

The flight was only a short hop and the 737 touched down at 10:01 a.m. Mac collected his suitcase and swiftly marched out of the concourse, trying to ease the ache in his knees. At the taxi rank, a slim forty-something Asian man pulled up in a 1989 Toyota Cressida with a sign on the roof saying Triangle Taxi's. Mac needed communications and a recce of what weapons were legally available. Instructing the driver of his need for a phone and a gun shop, the Asian said he knew of just the place for both.

"The Pavilion, just off N2, will have everything you need."

"The Pavilion?"

"Yes, it's a very new, very big shopping mall; everyone goes there. My name is Ravi," declared the driver, reaching over the seat to offer his hand.

A gun store in a shopping mall, now you've got to be kidding.

It didn't take Mac long to realise three things. One, they drive on the right just like the UK.

Becky will be pleased.

Two, he hadn't seen a single security camera on the streets.

Always a good sign.

Three, no-one took a blind bit of notice about the speed limit signs.

The driver passed over a copy of the local newspaper. Milosevic's death was still news, conspiracy theories were plentiful.

It says here that Milosevic died of a heart attack whilst being in isolation from the other prisoners at Scheveningen Prison?

Hah! so much for democracy and freedom of the press. They couldn't say that it was lax security at the Tribunal buildings, that would be just tooooo embarrassing. So, they moved him and said it

was simply a well-known heart condition that got unexpectedly worse. Well, there's a lot to be said for European subsidies and the fat cats who sit at the top of the tree collecting them.
Fuckin' hypocrites!!
Mac threw the paper away in disgust.

After fifteen minutes at warp three they arrived at the Pavilion. A huge shopping mall that looked like something out of a Jules Verne novel. Four large Crystal Palace-like towers atop a slogan-laden castle; it was impressive and a little surreal.

Ravi parked the Toyota outside Nandos restaurant and Mac went in search of equipment. It didn't take too long to arrange a pay-as-you-go mobile phone on Vodacom for 350 rand, around £35. He didn't have the same luck with the gun shop; after twenty minutes he asked at a security products store and was told it had closed down, as had many other gun shops under new government legislation. The only other one that the manager knew about was Kings, on Hunter Street.

Mac went back to the taxi and they trailed back the way they'd already come. Fortunately, the store wasn't far from the Southern Sun Elangeni hotel where Mac had a provisional reservation.

Parked outside the flat-topped building of Kings, Mac walked through the grilled main door and pressed the buzzer for entry; it clicked open.

The shop consisted of one rectangular room about ten metres by twenty, with an L-shaped serving counter along two walls. On the left wall were hunting lamps, crossbows and reloading equipment. Against the far, long wall were air rifles with airsoft pistols in cabinets beneath them. The shorter wall on the right held bolt-action and semi-automatic rifles and shotguns, with automatic pistols and revolvers in glass cabinets below. The last wall held accessories, telescopic truncheons, stun guns, pepper sprays and paintball guns. In the centre of the room were flat-topped glass cabinets holding various small folders and large hunting knives. Mac felt quite at home.

Mac took his time reading notices posted on the walls behind the counter. There had been a major change in government legislation ten months previously and all firearms now required a licence together with a competency course which must be successfully completed.

It's never made easy for me.

After his initial walk around Mac thought he'd see how far he could go with equipment, motioning for the six-foot-four, unshaved, spectacle-wearing guy whose name plate suggested he was called Rick, to help.

"Can I have one-hundred nine-mil hollow-points please?" Mac asked casually.

"What grain?" asked Rick in a deep South African accent, referring to the bullet head weight.

"Standard one-hundred and twenty-four grain if you have them."

"Sure, anything else?"

"I'll take two of the Blaser paintball guns, five-hundred yellow and two-hundred black paintballs. Two long distance pepper sprays, two Uzi stun guns – what voltage are they?"

"Seven hundred and fifty thousand volts, knocks 'em down real quick," Rick said with a knowing smile.

"Ok, and two extendable batons."

"That all, sir?"

Mac considered a decoy.

"I'll take a Lynx sixty-millimetre spotting scope as well thanks."

Rick took all the goods over to the till and calculated the prices.

"That'll be four thousand, one hundred rand sir."

Mac handed over the cash in two-hundred rand notes, took his purchases and went back to the waiting car.

After having paid off the taxi on the steps of the Elangeni hotel, Mac registered as Mathew Jones; unusually, they didn't ask to see his passport, and was escorted to his room on the fourth floor. With a twenty rand tip tucked inside his waistcoat pocket, the porter closed the door behind him. Mac looked at the plastic carrier bag full of equipment. He unpacked, showered and went to bed, sleeping for ten hours. At 8am the next morning he woke with two thoughts first, *Becky will be here tomorrow.*

Second, *Step two… preparation.*

•••

Hussein Kamal sat quietly in the Bayswater apartment, sipping Earl Grey tea with lemon. Swan Lake played quietly in the background through a pair of Panasonic speakers that cost more than Pakistan's national debt. There are times for action and times for inaction; for Kamal, this was neither.

At fifty-eight, Kamal had a good life, a wife he loved, two sons he adored, a well paid job as senior administration clerk with the Amn-Al Amn and Mukhabarat, Iraq's security services. Three years ago all that had changed when a car bomb intended for the occupying coalition security forces exploded in one of Baghdad's city suburbs. His entire family were gone in one fatal instant.

In his youth Kamal had been the family rebel, searching for answers to Islam and his own existence on earth by travelling first to Mecca on the Haj, the Muslim's holy pilgrimage, then to Afghanistan, where the American, then British troops subjugated his brethren. Initially by politics, then, once he realised this path was futile, by guns, bombs, death and destruction. Any method that would make the occupying forces listen to what he had to say. Kamal had killed more than his share of infidels and several of his own kind as well. If there was anything he hated more than an informer, he couldn't actually think what that could be. Kamal had found his best friend and close confidant Jalal had been passing on information to the security forces. Under extreme torture, he took three days to die, shackled to a cellar wall, his feet raw stumps of red flesh and still protesting his innocence. It had dismayed and upset Kamal to hurt his friend but that didn't stop him doing it.

The pen may be mightier than the sword everywhere else, but not in Afghanistan.

In the void after his family had been destroyed he was contacted. What had he to lose? Already everything that had meaning was gone, all that held him together was his faith, Islam.

At that fateful meeting, the mission he was asked to undertake had taken his breath away. The void he felt was filled with a new sense of purpose and direction. If he was successful he could re-pay all that Islam had given him, with interest.

One of the three pagers beeped, bringing Kamal's reverie to an end. Putting down his cup of tea he picked up the pager from the nearby table. The message read... AUNTY PAT GONE TO BINGO.

Kamal smiled thinly; this was the only message this pager would ever receive. He switched it off.

Each operative had a code word or phrase; each time a pager received a code, it meant that they were one step closer to the realisation of their dream, their objective.

Mobile phones could be traced, could be located to within three metres by triangulation from the receiving transponders that the phone had locked onto. Not so the pager; it only received messages, it did not transmit them and that was by radio signals, therefore, it could never give away its location.

They have thought of everything. I am the messenger, they are the planners. Once more they confirm we are followers of the superior faith.

Kamal switched on the wireless handset; it immediately connected to its base station sixty metres away in an empty apartment three floors up. The base station was connected by a standard BT landline to the telephone network. Above the phone, set into the coving was a small wireless video transmitter that relayed a signal to a receiver and 5 inch LCD screen that Kamal now checked.

If, and it was a very big if, one of the few calls he made was ever traced and the anti-terrorist services attacked the address to which it was registered, upstairs, Kamal would get prior warning that someone was on his trail via the LCD screen. A simple idea, virtually foolproof.

Truly we are the chosen ones.

The phone was answered on the third ring; Kamal smiled. *God is great.*

•••

No-one there, shit they're fast but it doesn't take a brain surgeon to figure out who's responsible for this.

John got down from his vantage point and went downstairs to phone a glazier. He didn't bother phoning the police, they never came to the estate for anything less than a dead body or major drug's bust.

The glazier arrived quicker than John would have expected, it appeared business was slow. John explained that he'd have to leave him to sort the mess out and to replace the glass on his own as he had to pick up his daughter from school.

"No problem mate. I'll be here a while anyway. I've seen the bricks, maybe when you get back you can tell me how it happened."

"Yeah. When I get back."

John met Rachael at the school gates and they walked unhurriedly back. While walking he explained what had happened and told her not to be scared.

"Scared Daddy? Why would I be scared with you here?" she was utterly serious; in the way only children can ever be.

The glazier had finished by 7pm. He'd done a good job too, John could see that. After calling at the house, Rachael had changed from her school clothes and John took her to a Chinese restaurant as a treat and to keep her out of the house. Rachael ordered her favourite, sweet and sour prawns with egg fried rice.

He tucked her into bed at 9.30, a little later than her usual bedtime, read her an extract from 'Survival under Artic Conditions' and kissed her on the forehead.

"Daddy? Will those bad men come back and smash our windows again?"

"No baby. But if they do, then I'll have to teach them a lesson; won't I?"

"Will it be a hard lesson Daddy?" she asked; snuggling into the pillow.

"Yes Angel, really hard."

"Good. Night night Daddy."

"Night night Angel."

He loved her so much it hurt.

chapter seven

Mac showered and dressed quickly. Twelve minutes later he was on the ground floor eating a full English breakfast in the hotel restaurant.

Collecting a copy of Durban's Yellow Pages from the concierge Mac planned his day. There were two further gun shops in the area, one at Game City, and Buccaneers in Victoria Street. Next, he needed maps of Drackensburg park and Cathedral Peak. He'd try the tourist information building at Tourist Junction.

Once he had looked these places over he would return to the hotel and use the business suite internet services. After that he would buy a car then sit in his room and collate all the information so far.

Mac picked up his small day-pack and headed out of the hotel's main doors and into the first taxi on the rank, via the hot South African sun.

"Game City in Greyville first, then Victoria Street, ok?" Mac settled in to the rear seat.

"Ok, sir." The driver spoke good English.

This was how Mac's life was, structured, organised. Once Becky had asked him to describe his life. "Ninety-nine percent boredom, one percent sheer panic." She'd laughed at his answer because she believed hers was the exact opposite.

In less than ten minutes they were at the group of buildings known as Game City; the driver said he'd wait in the car park. Mac walked through the corridors until he found "Blade and Bow." A grilled security wall separated the firearms section from the hunting bows and knives; here Mac made his first discovery. In a showcase he found several black powder revolvers with a handwritten sign saying 'NO LICENCE REQUIRED.'

Hmm, if nothing else these could come in handy.

Mac purchased two Pietta .36 calibre 1851 Navy Brass revolvers with seven and a half inch barrels and walnut grips. Four half-kilo packs of black powder and fifty .36 balls of ammunition. He was familiar with the loading process but still read the information leaflet that came with them. The Piettas would fire six chambers then would require reloading; this would take three to four minutes each time. The Piettas would only be used as a last resort.

As Tzun Tzu says, "always plan your escape first."

Mac had considered a crossbow but felt that there wouldn't be enough distance in the jungle where he could warrant carrying such a large and heavy piece of kit, and with the jungle being so dense a small twig or branch could easily deflect its flight. It was tempting to have a weapon that could fire a silent shot but he eventually declined.

Marrying up with the taxi, Mac called at the Buccaneer gun shop on Victoria Street but there was nothing that he could use here. On the way there he had noticed a sign on Beatrice Street saying 'Ndali Fireworks'; if he needed pyrotechnics he now knew where he could get them.

The next port of call was the Tourist Information office, barely a minute from Victoria Street. The female on duty was very helpful and Mac left with two maps of the area he was interested in. They were not as detailed as he would have liked but would do if nothing else was available.

Back at the hotel Mac sat on a leather sofa just off the main doors waiting for his kiwi tartlet and coffee, whilst he contemplated the day's events and progress.

"Can I be intrusive and sit here?"

Mac looked up at the dark-haired woman dressed in a white trouser suit, small prince-nez style glasses perched on the end of her pert nose.

"Of course," Mac replied, jolted from his mental machinations.

The mid-thirties woman plonked herself down on the sofa just as her mobile rang. As she was talking Mac gleaned that she was called Denise and was a visa and immigration consultant. Mac ordered coffee for them both, she finished on the phone.

"Thanks for the coffee; I needed to pee," she drawled in a strong South African accent.

"What?" Mac thought he'd misunderstood.

"The hotel is halfway between the American Embassy and my office but I didn't think I'd make it, so I came here for a pee." She beamed a dazzling confident smile.

She was earthy, direct; Mac liked her straightaway. She told him she was married, had two children and had been having an affair for six years with another married man, her boss. They discussed politics; Mac learned of the huge increase in crime; smash and grab of personal effects when parked at 'robots.' Mac worked out that robots were the South African name for traffic lights. Denise talked of government corruption and the recent death of Brett Kebble. Mac played dumb but knew more about the incident than he could say.

Brett Kebble had been driving home at 9.15pm in his silver S-class Mercedes; he had parked at Atholl-Oaklands on a bridge above Johannesburg's M1 motorway. Four nine-millimetre rounds hit the Merc from close-range, one killed Kebble instantly. A multi-millionaire, Kebble had helped create two of South Africa's four largest gold producers.

After his death the 41-year-old's accounts were audited; almost four billion rand (£400 million) was missing and couldn't be traced.

Less than seven people in the world knew the truth;. Kebble, an ANC member and closet political activist, owned a company called sxr Uranium One. He had approached the Polish Mafia with a view to purchasing sufficient radioactive material to make a nuclear bomb. Small enough to fit in a briefcase, large enough to level a city the size of London. Kebble could have made almost any demand that would further the political power struggle in South Africa and beyond.

Action 6 could not allow this, a bigger version of the July 7th London bombings, to go ahead.

Mac had originally been briefed for the job but with the advent of securing the Prime Minister's assassination, withdrew.

Another operative took Mac's place, was briefed to make it look like a criminal event – break-in, mugging or drive-by shooting. Kebble, once on Action 6's list, never stood a chance and would pay the ultimate price for his folly and grandiose ideas.

With Kebble's demise the Uranium232 deal fell through and the Polish Mafia knew when they were being sent a message.

Denise's phone pinged a second time; someone wanted a visa to travel to Spain.

Once she'd finished, it was time for her to go back to the office. Fishing in her purse she pulled out a shopping list and scribbled down her cellphone number and e-mail address on its reverse.

"You know, everyone gets lonely now and again." She smiled, leant over and kissed Mac's cheek, got up and walked out of the hotel.

It wasn't often that Mac was nonplussed but this was one of those times.

He sat there for a few minutes gathering his thoughts. He knew he was no Robert Redford, knew too that for a woman to hand over her number like that was unusual.

She could be South African Intelligence, local undercover operative or... just lonely. She's right, everyone needs someone now and again.

Mac looked at the shopping list a fraction too long.

Becky will be here tomorrow.

With that final thought Mac put the list in his pocket, walked upstairs to the internet room and went back to work.

chapter eight

Becky arrived at Durban airport a little after 10am.

With her sun-kissed shoulders, well-honed body and long raven hair she was the centre of a hormone storm. One guy, smartly dressed, was so taken by Becky's muscled calves and enigmatic smile, he didn't notice the elderly lady pulling a light-blue suitcase until he tripped arse over tit. He was quite acrobatic; as he fell forward and over, his eyes never left Becky's face.

Becky managed to be both graceful and ungainly at the same time. Anyone who looked closely would notice that at no time did she bump into anyone or allow the fast moving crowd to impede her swift progress. It evolved from the training she had received from Mac and was based on the samurai code. If one samurai warrior's sword scabbard 'accidentally,' or otherwise touched another samurai's sword scabbard it would be considered the ultimate insult and a fight to the death would inevitably follow. Mac had shown her how to 'see' everyone and everything around her, to be aware, and it would look to others as though her ability to move through the morass of people was simply good fortune. One more observant fellow sat resting on a bench, a keen deep-sea fisherman. Becky caught his peripheral vision and he was visibly startled from his sojourn.

My God. For a moment I thought the girl in the black dress was a shark bearing down on me. But my, she is rather fetching.

The perceptive man followed Becky's rear as she made her way through the immigration hall and out into the main concourse.

Makes me wish I was twenty years and one coronary younger.

He slapped his knee and laughed so hard he convulsed in a fit of coughing.

As she moved forward she saw a man holding a square of corrugated cardboard with "Miss Becky" emblazoned in thick blue felt tip.
"I'm Becky."
The black man doffed his cap.
"May I take your case?"
"Sure." Becky passed him the handle.
"Please follow me. My name is Jasper, I am to take you to the Southern Sun Elangeni hotel," said the driver in rapid-fire English.
Outside in the taxi rank was a white Mercedes. Becky got in. Fifteen minutes later she had registered and was unpacking her change of clothes as the phone rang.
"Yup."
"Don't you yup me in that tone young lady," Mac jibed.
"Yeah, yeah," she laughed, "where are you?"
"Room four-ten."
"Be there in a jiffy."
After cradling the phone Becky sat on the bed for a moment.
He just calls and I come running. He just clicks his fingers and I fly half-way round the world. Who does he think he is? He's... I'll bet he's got me something nice and I'll bet whatever we're goin' to do is dangerous.
Becky stood up and clapped her hands excitedly.
Goody!!

Mac waited for Becky to arrive at his room. He was glad she'd made it ok; he worried about her when she wasn't around, but then, he worried about her when she was around too.
Mac had a very busy day yesterday. The internet searches had taken longer than expected and he still couldn't find a decent map of the Cathedral Peak area. After the searches he had walked to Lion Pride Used Cars and bought a two-year old Freelander for 169,000 rand with a secured MasterCard on a Swiss Bank. He'd

also revisited some of the shops and bought a few additional items, including two-way radios with boom microphones.

Although Mac was expecting her, Becky still used the agreed door knock: once, twice then a quick double tap. Mac opened the door and despite telling herself that she wouldn't, Becky melted into his arms. Mac kissed her on the cheek, holding onto her for slightly longer than was customary. He held her cheeks, brushed her hair.

He loves me, I love him. It would never work between us, never, never... never?

"You're glad to see me then," she grinned. A Cheshire cat wouldn't have had a look in.

"Of course I'm glad." Mac remonstrated. "Last time you left, I noticed your forward roll needed working on, we'll sort that out."

Becky pulled away and punched Mac's shoulder.

"That's more like it," he said, wincing, rubbing his arm theatrically.

Becky brushed passed Mac, glancing at herself in the wall mirror as she did so. Something was different. She hadn't been wearing earrings, now she was. Looking closer, Becky swept back her raven hair.

"Tanzanite!" she exclaimed.

"Oh, so now you notice. I always thought you were the quick one." He laughed.

The large two-carat deep-blue Tanzanite earrings in a claw setting sparkled with lustre.

"They're..."

"Beautiful, magnificent, fantastic, colourful and without equal?"

"Yes," decided Becky honestly, still looking at herself in the mirror.

"Then I was right, they do suit you."

Becky kicked off her shoes and jumped up and down on the bed like an over-excited child. Having changed into a tight orange sleeveless top and short skirt, she giggled.

"Where's your Spectre?" asked Mac accusingly, suddenly serious.

Becky stopped bouncing, raised the denim skirt to her waist. There, clipped to a pair of white panties with pink heart motifs was the Spectre. She unclipped it and flicked it open.

"See." She laughed.

"Yeah, too much for an old man like me." Mac shook his head, he couldn't help but laugh.

Becky bounced again then dived towards Mac, who caught her.

"You could see more if you wanted," she said in a husky, sultry voice.

Mac took in her steady gaze, swollen lips, dark alluring eyes. He gulped unexpectedly.

"What did you have in mind?" he asked, as casually as he possibly could.

This was dangerous ground, ground they'd long ago agreed would never be walked on. Becky leant fractionally forward, her lips almost touching his ear.

"This," she whispered seductively.

Pushing Mac with her left hand, her right threw the Spectre, spinning upward. Turning 180 degrees and taking one step forward, her right hand moved to the base of her spine. She looked in one direction and caught the spinning Spectre by the handle blindly behind her back. Becky's right hand flew forward and the knife embedded into the fire regulations on the door, two full knife-spins away.

THUD!

Becky clapped her hands with glee, then proceeded to extricate the knife.

Mac was doubly pleased; firstly with Becky's prowess and secondly, with the fact that she had tricked him.

I should have expected something after I'd slipped the earrings on her.

"See," she said, returning and folding the knife. "I'm getting better, aren't I?"

Mac smiled in a fatherly way, "Yes little one, you certainly are." And stroked her cheek.

"What's the food like here?" Her mood changed rapidly.

"Let's go and find out shall we?" He held out his arm, taking her mood swing in his stride.

"Ok." She linked him.

It had almost gone wrong. When Becky had looked into his eyes she had nearly forgotten to throw the knife, nearly kissed him. That would have certainly ruined the bond they shared, the life they had together.

He loved her; she knew it.

chapter nine

Henry Bishop sat at his twin-terminaled computer, hands acting independently on each of the keyboards. Henry had worked for various government security agencies for most of his life. Deep within the bowels of Whitehall, Henry and his secretary Helen worked to help keep secure the British way of life. The door sign said 'The Director of Finance and Control' but Henry was more than that, much more. Henry, known universally as the 'Director', had a simple world-wide mandate. To take murderous action against any corporate, government or individual who threatened Britain's security or, retrospectively, to mete out punishment to those that had already taken such actions.

Only one person knew of the Director and his true purpose: the Prime Minister. Taking the position since the previous PM's assassination six months ago, so far, he had not called on the Director's services but that did not matter. Henry's mandate was autonomous, he needed no authorisation or sanction for any actions he took.

The organisation was designated 'Action 6'; its operatives, never more than six. Each operative worked alone, never meeting with any other from the organisation, each one above the law, each one deniable.

Reports from MI5, MI6, Special Branch and the Secret Intelligence Services were diverted from their original destinations, siphoned to pass through Henry's terminals, then re-routed to their intended recipient.

Henry had been following closely the apparent murders and accidental deaths of several upper-class and titled figures over a number of months. Whilst at first disturbing, as more were killed, the latest being Lady Wainwright and Angus McDougal, the strategy became more obvious.

"Someone, somewhere is killing off those in the line of succession to the throne."

Why?

"I don't know." Henry, as a consequence of working alone for many years, would answer his own thoughts verbally. Henry thought nothing of this, it was simply his way of organising his thoughts, not any form of schizophrenia.

What could their criteria possibly be?

"I don't know that either."

Henry's fingers skipped over the dual keyboards, sometimes just a blur, accessing reports and secret databases. An hour later Henry stopped and rubbed the bridge of his nose then his temples, wearily.

"According to the information, other than second cousins and other remote descendents, there are only twelve people left in direct line of succession."

If all these people are killed off... what then? Who fills the void?

Henry pressed the intercom button.

"Helen, please come in."

Helen, Henry's long-time secretary entered the inner sanctum. She looked like the archetypal schoolteacher that everyone remembered in fond memories. Five foot five, long greying brown hair pulled tightly back in a bun, bright intelligent inquisitive eyes that missed nothing. Helen lived at home with four cats and a display of medals from her undercover activities living, working and breathing as part of an IRA active cell. How many lives she had saved by relaying information to the Intelligence Services was anyone's guess. Pen and paper at the ready, she pulled up a chair and sat waiting for instructions. Henry turned from the monitors.

"There's something going on here, my dear. Something that I still don't fully understand." Helen sat poised with the pen.

"Members of the Royal Family and several connected members in the line of succession to the throne have been assassinated." Helen looked up, locked eyes, waiting.

"I need all the operatives to be aware of the situation. I want them to report any rumblings, any information, no matter how minuscule, anything even remotely connected."

Helen had never seen the Director with spittle on his lips before.

This must really be a serious situation.

Helen sat back in her own office. Memorised e-mail addresses were sent a breakdown of the situation. The e-mails were routed then re-routed through security service communication channels, then through virtual offices and large company organisations. It was completely untraceable, completely sterile.

Helen contemplated the fervour and passion with which the Director, normally detached from decisions, had instructed her.

I've never seen him so... agitated. But, I suppose if someone's threatening the Royal Family and the succession, maybe he has a right to feel so strongly. This is more than a job to him, it's his life.

The screen fanfared 'e-mail sent ok.' Helen pondered a moment longer then went back to wrapping a birthday present for Oscar. He would be four next Saturday and, of all her cats, was the favourite.

●●●

Mac and Becky left the hotel at 7am. Both dressed in shorts, black T-shirts and Hi-Tech lightweight boots. They walked over the road and onto the beach promenade where they turned right and began to jog.

"How far we goin'?" asked Becky.

"See the maritime communications tower on the bluff? There and back, only we come back on the sand."

"Ok."

It wasn't a race, more of an acclimatisation jog, get the pores working, get used to the humidity.

"Cameras," said Becky pointing upward.

"Yeah, they're only on the beach promenade, none in town or anywhere else. See the guy over there with the cowboy hat? He's just there to hold people's car keys and stop the cars from being broken into. There's a lot of crime in South Africa, Durban in particular."

Just then a pair of motorcycle cops passed, going in the opposite direction.

"What were they carrying?"

"Both had Berretta 92Fs."

"Anything else?"

"Yeah," said Becky sarcastically "an extra twenty pounds each, all of it round the gut."

After four-hundred metres the promenade abruptly stopped, mesh barriers obstructed their progress. Turning right up to the marine parade they continued parallel to the beach.

The promenade started again at Ushaka Marine World, a complex of waterfalls, water slides and a real Dutch cruiser in which the stern metal plates had been replaced with smoked sun-proof windows. Mac could just make out tables with white cloths inside.

Probably a restaurant.

Helicopter charter was advertised; Mac made a mental note of the telephone number.

You never know... 082 390 3566.

Twenty-seven minutes later they reached the base of the bluff. Without respite Mac turned and ran down to the beach; without hesitation, Becky followed.

"Everytime I do a forward roll, you take ten paces and do one too, ok?"

"Ok."

Mac leant forward without breaking stride and launched himself; spinning onto the back of his right shoulder, taking the roll diagonally along to his left hip, he came up onto his feet and continued to jog in one smooth motion.

Becky took ten paces then copied the same manoeuvre; she wasn't quite as fluid as Mac but still managed to regain her feet and continue jogging.

Every two to three hundred metres was a concrete pier, used by the early surfers as a means of getting past the waves, by jumping off the end of it. The only other beach occupants were a few sleeping figures under gaudy coloured blankets and the early sand sculptors setting their naked ladies, horses and lions with spray moisture in the expectation of a few rand thrown into a handkerchief by passing tourists.

During the beach jog they did thirty rolls each; sand got everywhere.

"Ok, stop." They were both sweating freely but not yet out of breath.

"Assume a ready position, block and throw." Without hesitation Mac threw an open-hand 'shuto' strike to Becky's face. She instinctively double-blocked with her right hand, gripped his wrist with her left, followed the block and spun into Mac as her right hand continued to Mac's right shoulder. She hit Mac in the crotch with her bottom then, still holding onto his shoulder, dropped vertically to her knees, dragging his wrist downwards at the same time.

With the block then the distraction of a hit to his crotch, Mac's hips moved back an instinctive fraction out of harm's way. This had the effect of breaking his balance and pushing his shoulders forward. With Becky dropping vertically, Mac's shoulder was pulled downwards and over Becky's head. He couldn't do anything about it so went with the throw. Landing on his back, Mac followed through, continuing the impetus, rolled and came up into a ready stance. As he did so he turned on the balls of his feet to face Becky who was coming at him from her crouched position, like a tigress protecting her cubs.

Her 'Ippon Seonage' or one-arm-shoulder-throw had been almost perfect but she had released him too soon and Mac was able to roll away.

Mac quickly moved forward catching Becky off guard and duplicated the move, only this time he held onto her as she landed in the sand. Just as her back hit the floor he leant forward, moving his right arm around her neck and grabbing his own left hand. Using his chest, Mac pressed the back of Becky's head, forcing her chin over the strangulation hold, using her own body to lock his arm into position against her throat. This was known as the "Vhin ha torq" strangulation hold, a Vietnamese speciality. Becky tried to reach his eyes or any other vulnerable point but already she was growing weaker as her brain was starved of oxygen; she patted Mac's arm, and he released her.

"See the difference?"

Becky rubbed her neck.

"Yeah. Hold onto the assailant a fraction longer."

"That's right." Mac held out his hand and helped Becky up.

"What now?" she asked, brushing sand from her hair and clothing.

"How about a shower and full English breakfast?"

"With black pudding?" she asked excitedly, eyes wide open.

"We can but try, little one," Mac added as he kissed her on the forehead. "We can but try."

After breakfast and before meeting Becky in his room, Mac had checked his PGP encrypted e-mail account and read the situation report that Helen had sent. He hadn't heard anything that was even remotely connected to the Royal family but would keep his ears open for any developments.

Becky had devoured breakfast, disappointed at there not being any black pudding but consoled herself that there were two types of bacon and three types of mushrooms.

When Becky arrived, Mac had laid a copy of the Daily Sun on the bed. On it were the two Piettas.

"Pay attention." Mac was in instructor mode.

"New legislation has negated the supply of modern firearms and our time frame does not allow for such weapons to be appropriated. These are what I have managed to procure. Point 36 calibre 1851 Navy Brass six-shot black powder revolvers." Mac passed one to Becky, which surprised her as she wasn't wearing gloves.

"Here in South Africa, these are completely legal."

Becky hefted the revolver; it was very heavy indeed and a lot more shiny than she was used to seeing.

Not that much different from a Desert Eagle automatic and that was really heavy.

"There's no requirement for you to know how to load it, as once we set off all we will have is six shots each. We won't have a facility for reloading, ok?"

"Ok."

Mac pulled out one of the stun guns from his daypack.

"We have one of these each. Seventy-five thousand volts; one to four seconds and the enemy is dazed, he'll fall to the ground but be able to recover quite quickly. Aim for the neck or torso and hold it there for five seconds. He will be semi-conscious and dazed, unable to move for ten or fifteen minutes, ok?"

"Ok."

"Any questions so far?"

Becky paused, shook her head.

"No questions."

This was the way Mac always gave his orders to Becky: succinct, terse. That way she only had to remember enough to do her part, nothing more. Mac called it 'compartmentalisation.'

"We have one each of these pepper-sprays. Good for humans and animals. Just in case there are dogs in the area. We'll be moving out the day after tomorrow, travelling in the Freelander that you'll get a chance to drive in the morning. It's a three hour drive to the Cathedral Peak Hotel in the Drakensburg nature reserve area just short of the Lesotho border. I'll show you the route later.

"I've got a set of camo gear and belt equipment for you, familiarise yourself with it tonight. We'll book into the hotel as dirty old man and bit of rough."

Becky smiled.

No change there then.

"The same night we'll head out over the border, about four miles north-west, until we hit the Orange River. We'll be on foot, in a jungle environment for two to five days. I'll have given the hotel a story about searching for rare butterflies.

"We'll have radio comms between ourselves but our mobiles," Mac handed her one, "will be switched off. I don't expect there will be a signal but they may come in handy for an emergency on the exfiltration, ok?"

"Ok."

"We'll set up an observation post. We're looking for a small boat using a silent electric motor. Once we see where it docks, I will infiltrate; you will be my cover.

"Any questions?"

Becky paused again.

"How long will the infiltration take?"

"Not known. I would hope to be in and out in less than two hours but you will wait for twelve. If I don't return, make your way back to the hotel and make like we had an argument. If I'm not back within twelve hours of you being at the hotel, take the Freelander, go to the airport and fly home. I'll contact you as soon as I can."

"Enemy forces?"

"Once we leave the Cathedral Peak Hotel we avoid all contact. On the infiltration, it's likely that there will be armed guards with night-vision goggles and sensors. I don't really know for sure, it's something we'll have to play by ear. Anything else?"

Becky thought for a moment.

"Medical?"

"I'll have a full med kit in my bergan which I'll leave with you in the OP when I do the infiltration. Anything else?"

"No."

"Right, listen closely, there's a few 'Actions On' that I want to go through."

chapter ten

Kensington Dalyrimple-Plantagenet was a lot more pretentious than his name suggested, far more. Middle-aged and dressed in a pale blue suit with a peacock yellow lining, it was, undoubtedly an Oswald Boateng original, costing almost two-thousand pounds. Add to this a shirt from Jermyn Street in London, with matching tie and kerchief and shoes from Tricker's where he'd had his own personal last made. Each pair of shoes was handmade and took sixteen weeks to finish. The pair he currently wore were black brogues with a thick rubber sole adding slightly to his height. He was six-feet tall and slim, with mannerisms that could best be described as feminine, but more accurately, should they have an unusual grasp of the English language, they would have used a word no longer considered to have current usage. Some two-hundred years ago, he would have been labelled a fop. Someone who could reel off the rules of etiquette for a dinner evening but who had no job or sense of purpose other than to gossip or look good. He would request of anyone who cared to listen, that he wished to be referred to as Ken, as he thought this made him more approachable and one of the common crowd. The main distinguishing feature, that everyone spoke about when describing him, was not his fashionably over-the ear black hair, nor his neat features and moustache, which he thought was very Errol Flynn, but in fact was more Terry-Thomas. No, it was the ten-inch long brushed steel cigarette holder that he invariably carried. Ken smoked around thirty cigarettes a day but, as you would expect from someone of his ilk, they were hand-rolled Turkish cigarettes sold only in Istanbul and flown over six times a year for him personally by a man who owed Ken his very life.

Ken was at this moment in Edinburgh spending a half hour perusing the shops along the Royal Mile whilst waiting for a meeting at one of the nearby hotels. Ken didn't so much walk as sashay like some sixteenth-century courtesan with nothing to kill but time.

Ken was an arms dealer and, by all accounts, a very good one. The vast majority of his deals were on the African continent, but he was not averse to broadening his horizons and considered every country fair game. The person he was meeting today was from Ethiopia and had ten thousand Kalashnikovs and twenty thousand POMZ-2 Russian hand grenades to sell.

He'll be the usual type. Some kind of minister in the military junta, maybe a self-styled general with enough medals and braid to circumnavigate the globe. Someone who wants to rape his own country of its meagre resources and set himself up in a penthouse suite with a mistress. In a couple of months he'll have squandered all the money he's made and his countrymen will still be living in shit with no electricity or clean running water. Welcome to the capitalist society where every man's money is welcome, no matter how dirty.

He checked his watch, a Jaeger-Le-Couture diamond-encrusted indulgence that lay heavy on his thin wrist. He smiled knowingly to himself at his own excess.

Who am I to judge?

Ken had been brought up in minor aristocracy. He'd been born in England but moved to France at the age of six to be looked after by his great-grandmother who insisted he spoke only French in the large manor house. He was enrolled in a local school and, because of his language difficulties, was bullied by the local children who hated the English immigrant with the atrocious accent. As the months became years, Ken studied by day and worked on the manor farm in the evenings, weekends and school holidays. During his time at the manor house Ken discovered that his father had lost the family home and estate through his gambling addiction. Once he'd lost everything, he killed himself but only after he'd murdered his wife too. Ken wasn't sure if his grandmother blamed him in some way for her daughter's death. It wasn't something that was ever discussed. He never really knew his father very well and now that he'd found out the truth, was sorry he had. It was much better to believe that his father was a world-renowned scientist or entrepreneur. Anything but the stark reality.

Ken's life changed suddenly one balmy August night when he was fifteen years old.

While reading in his bedroom, Ken heard his grandmother cry out in alarm and he swiftly made his way to the library where he knew she would be, sitting knitting and rocking in her old chair. He was greeted by two burly unkempt men who looked as though they had been living rough. What Ken didn't know was that these two men had escaped from a police station in Paris nearly three weeks ago and had been sleeping in fields or wherever they could. By mugging and burglary they had managed to keep themselves fed but their money had run out and they saw the manor house as a way of providing funds to last them a while. They had his grandmother held in a tight grip around her shoulders and were demanding, in coarse gutter-French, to be told where the family jewels were kept. She couldn't tell them there were no such jewels; they wouldn't have believed her. Their manner was openly aggressive and Ken immediately feared for her life. He had been involved in a few small scuffles at school, nothing even remotely serious and would later find it difficult to accurately relate what he did next.

Taking in the scene before him Ken strode purposefully to the large open fireplace and grabbed a long iron poker. Without pause he took three steps to the first man holding his grandmother and cleaved his skull in one powerful swinging blow. The man dropped like a stone, grey brain matter spraying the velvet wallpaper on the far side of the room. The second thug was not so brave on his own and raised his hands in defence but to no avail. Ken held the iron rod like a pikestaff and drove it unceremoniously through the man's Adam's apple. His grandmother would never forget the look on her grandson's face as the second gypsy writhed on the floor trying desperately to pull out the poker from his throat and bleeding profusely in dark red spurts. Ken was calm, serene and unflustered, his eyes slightly glazed and seemingly focused on something far away. It was exactly the same curious look he had on his face when he read a book…

Grandmother took charge after the incident. She carefully cleaned up the blood on the wooden floor and walls, burning the rags afterwards in the roaring fire. Then, with Ken's help, they rolled each body into a carpet and dragged it out into the fields where they were both buried in deep graves. They swore they would never mention the incident and they never had. But that day something was permanently changed in Ken and no-one ever bullied him again.

•••

It was going well, better than expected, thought the man occupying the large white leather sofa. He was wearing neatly-pressed Armani trousers, brown belt and gold Gucci buckle. The tailored Pink shirt was a little too tight but not so that it spoiled the overall effect. No, what spoiled the overall effect was the Miss Piggy slippers that he habitually wore around the Dortmund penthouse apartment.

He was bald, with a beard longer than the prescribed 'width of a man's hand.' He no longer mingled with his countrymen nor attended daily prayer, so it didn't matter. Nothing mattered except the mission.

He didn't know where the boy was being held; he didn't want to know. It was of no consequence; wherever it was would be secure and comfortable.

He would be almost nine years old now. With his mother's nose and his father's colouring, no-one would dispute his parentage and even if they did, a DNA test would not lie.

Mustafa would have preferred to live in a warmer country but it was not his decision to make. Germany in April was cold, another reason why he didn't venture far, if at all.

Mustafa was pleased with the telephone call he had received. Not every assassination was broadcast on the FDR news.

Kamal was a good soldier. He did as he was told, nothing more. It's a pity we had to destroy his family to put him in the right frame of mind to accept God's work but it is for the greater good. The greater Islamic good.

Allah made me his vassal and I made Kamal mine.

Mustafa had activated two more sleeper cells via Kamal; if anything went wrong the authorities would follow leads only as far as the messenger.

As added insurance Mustafa was also receiving the signal from the wireless video transmitter three floors above Kamal. It was boosted and sent to a Belkin USB receiver, translated into a computer signal and transmitted via the internet, in real time, to the monitor on Mustafa's desk. If the authorities did trace Kamal, Mustafa would know and detonate the ten pounds of Semtex under Kamal's floorboards by mobile phone. Any tracking could go no further.

Yes, Kamal is a good soldier, expendable but good.
All praise to Allah for he truly moves in mysterious ways.

●●●

"Did you get the results?"

"Yeah. Cost me an arm and a leg but they appear to be accurate."

"So, come on, spill the beans." He said impatiently.

The taller of the two men laid out several sheets of A4 paper on the chipped wooden kitchen table.

"See here," he pointed to a spike on the chart. "It shows there was only one unaccounted call made, and the timing is just about perfect."

"What does that mean?" asked the man, unconsciously rubbing his injured leg.

"That call was for less than three seconds, enough to say a word like 'go' for instance. It's probable that the receiver of that call initiated the three distraction devices." He pulled another chart from the layout.

"See here," he said pointing. "The phone that received the call was in the area of a village called Broadland Row in Essex. This other chart shows that three other mobile phones initiated the explosions only seconds after receipt of the call. Then almost immediately all the phones were switched off and have never showed on any of the mobile networks since."

"So, what's next?"

"We go to Broadland Row, have a shufti at the layout, see what's there and have a talk to the locals."

"It's not much to go on."

"Got a better idea?" said the taller man now with an authoritarian edge to his voice.

"No, you're right. Let's see if this gets us any closer to the bastard."

"Good. Saddle up; we move in twenty."

●●●

After watching episode four of season four. The one where an armed gang of criminals take over a red London double-decker bus and take the civilians hostage. At the end of a very unprofessional stake-out, where everyone wears a white ear-piece, even the black team member. The would-be arms dealer and Walter Mitty type leads Red Troop to a business park. Here is where the hostage is held and a hilarious firefight ensues. When Henno; Red Troop's sergeant hears the gun fight between the two groups of rival criminals he exclaims that he could tell it was an AK firing because of the crack and thump. John couldn't help but explode into laughter as any fool knows there's crack and thump with any high-velocity weapon.

It would have made more sense to say he could recognise the particular rat-a-tat that an AK makes. It's quite unique.

The series had the desired effect and lifted his spirits. When it had finished John checked the doors and windows to ensure they were secure and retired to bed at 10.45pm.

At 1.36am he woke abruptly to the sound of splintering glass and a whooshing noise followed quickly by Rachael's scream. He dived out of bed naked and ran to his little girl's room, smashing it open in his haste. The room was ablaze: with his daughter's bed in the middle of the flames, Rachael was sat up in bed screaming. For John there was no choice in fact; he never considered any other action. He dived through the flames and onto the bed; scooped up Rachael then; using the mattress as a springboard jumped back over the flames and onto the upstairs landing. Still naked he ran down the stairs four at a time, through the kitchen and out of the rear door into the large walled garden. John looked over the roof at the flames licking the gutters on the opposite side of the building. It wouldn't be too long before it took a serious hold and spread to next door but he could already hear the sirens of the approaching fire engines. They'd get it under control in quick-time.

"Daddy?" asked the little voice held tightly against his chest.

"Are you hurt? Are you ok Angel?" John looked down at the little bundle held firm in his grasp.

"Yes Daddy I'm ok, honest. It's just...I have to ask you something," she said a little uncertainly.

"What Angel?" he replied absently, stroking her face and hair.

"Will...will you be teaching those bad men a hard lesson now?"

"Yes Angel," his voice tightened and his eyes turned to flint. "I will."

Rachael murmured as she snuggled into his warm chest and closed her eyes.

"Goody."

chapter eleven

Over the last two days Mac had kept Becky busy with training: driving, shooting, communication and patrolling skills and close quarter combat.

On the day's shooting, it quickly became apparent that using the loading chart's recommended black powder charge made the gun too powerful for close work. The recoil meant that multiple shots went high. Mac lowered the load so that it was consistent with sub-sonic nine-millimetre loads of 850 feet per second. To further reduce the awesome blast of these nineteenth-century weapons Mac stretched a number of elastic bands five inches from the end of the barrel, until they were a ball size of about an inch and a quarter in diameter. He then attached a regular size plastic coke bottle surrounded by black masking tape. The barrel went inside the coke bottle and the coke bottle neck was pressed firmly into the elastic ball, then secured in place with a metal pipe clasp tightened as far as possible. The coke bottle was packed with wire wool from scouring pads; it would only suppress a few rounds but the Piettas were only ever going to fire six rounds each, so that wasn't an issue. Mac had test fired the improvised silencer; it was bulky but remarkably effective.

They made Cathedral Peak Hotel in good time. Becky sat in the passenger seat either talking, counting telegraph poles, looking for exotic birds or eating food from the hamper Mac had arranged from the hotel Elangeni. He'd told them it was for six people; he'd gauged it just about right.

Mac had watched as the bush and woodland changed to subtropical jungle; the change had been so gradual as to be almost imperceptible.

The Cathedral Peak Hotel was a testament to one man's vision, Albert van der Riet. At the turn of the century the area was owned by a farmer called Buys. Albert encouraged the farmer to sell, he was having problems with the San natives, more commonly called 'Bushmen.' The first building was a small cottage in which Albert and his family lived while the hotel was being built. The first bedding stones were laid in 1936. Looking like a cross between mock Tudor and a Swiss chalet it was impressive, made even more so by its location, almost a million miles from anywhere, or so it seemed.

The Basotho stonemasons really strutted their stuff on this place. And when you remember that there wasn't even a road or even major track to this location way back then, their feat is even more remarkable.

Becky summed it up in her usual succinct manner.

"Nice place. When we gonna eat?"

They booked in at the large reception hall; Mac carried the bergan, allowing the smartly dressed porter the suitcases.

Never get separated from your kit.

In their large four-poster bedded honeymoon suite Mac tipped the sweating porter and put his bergan on the bed. The porter pocketed the tip. Mac recognised the all-knowing-smile displayed on the porter's face; their subterfuge had worked yet again.

At least he had the courtesy not to give me the usual all-knowing-wink. Human nature is truly constant, it's unconstrained by continental borders. What's true in Belgium is still valid in South Africa. Hey, I'm a dirty-old-man on at least two continents.

While Becky wandered around the room looking at the ornaments, seeing how the curtains were stitched and feeling the pile of the carpet, Mac did a final check of the equipment. Insisting they get a few hours rest before they started on the route-in, Becky didn't argue and snuggled into Mac as they lay on the king-size bed, his arm around her shoulders. It wasn't long before her breathing became shallow as she drifted into sleep.

Mac lay awake for a while, going over the meeting he'd had with Norman at the Presidential Suite in Beirut.

As Dick and Dom left the suite, Mac put the Spectre back into his waistband.

"Now," he said with authority, "what do you want of me?"

Norman steepled his fingers, paused, deciding how to play the meet; in the end he decided that the truth would serve him better than any lie.

"There is a man who has become synonymous with the plight of the Muslim cause. He commands a vast network of intelligence gatherers, spies and volunteers willing to do his bidding, even at the expense of their own lives. He has been a recluse for many years, directing operations from secret locations through intermediaries and other like-minded organisations. He has made many enemies, most notably the United States of America, and more recently Western Europe, Spain and the United Kingdom especially." Norm paused for breath and leant forward and lowered his voice conspirationally.

"He is known by many names, his most recent, a name that inflames the media, a name that is linked to just about every terrorist attack that hits the western headlines. In the east he is called 'The Saviour,' in the west he's known as… Osama Bin Laden."

Mac leant back and assimilated what Norm had just said.

Shit. This is the big one.

"What of this man? What is he to me?" Mac acted impatient, his heart beating loudly in his ears.

Unperturbed, Norm continued.

"President Bush has pledged three billion dollars to help with Lebanese integration; help us move into the 21st century. Have you any idea of what this will mean?"

Mac remained silent; the question was rhetorical.

"Schools will receive the books they need, new housing for the families living ten to a room. Hotels and redesigned beach areas and facilities for tourism; these funds will transform my country, propel it towards its rightful place as the jewel of the Middle-East. We need this money, we will have this money." Norm added fervently.

"The US isn't just going to give you these funds without some assurances," Mac stated matter-of-factly. "What is it they want?"

Here it comes.

"They want Osama Bin Laden to retire; dismantle his Al-Qaeda network. He can live out his days in the Bekka Valley unmolested and without fear of reprisal."

"And if he won't do that?"

"Then you are to kill him," Norm said with finality.

Mac stood up, walked over to the large windows overlooking the remnants of the St George Hotel, the crater where President Hariri was assassinated still clearly visible.

"I have a few questions." Mac continued to stare through the window, then turned.

"How do I find Osama?"

"I do not know... but I may know someone who does. Several weeks ago Khalid Rashid was abducted from his Estcourt home in South Africa. Rashid is known by another name, one you will be more familiar with... Abu Musab al-Zarqawi, Osama's right hand man."

"Zarqawi is in Jordan, in hiding."

"No. The photograph printed by the newspapers is of another Jordanian citizen who masquerades as Zarqawi to confuse the intelligence services."

"Why would a man put his life on the line like that?"

"I do not know the specifics but his family is being held; they are safe as long as he evades capture. Rashid was a suspect in the Indonesian bombing but he was not involved in this; the South African police thought otherwise. His details were passed on to the American embassy. A short time later he disappeared."

"Where to?"

"We believe he is being held in an extraordinary rendition camp in Lesotho, in the mountains at the beginning of the Orange River just west of the South African border."

"How did they get him there?"

"A silent boat makes the trip at the end of each month. We do not know the camp's exact location but it is a very small compound, holding no more than twenty prisoners, probably less. The Americans do not know Rashid's true identity and it's unlikely he will ever tell them, but he may die under torture and we have no other link to Osama. Time is of the essence, I'm afraid."

"So, let me get this right." Mac paced. "I have to rescue Osama Bin Laden's right hand man from a fortified American Rendition camp at an undisclosed location in the middle of the jungle. Get him to tell me where Osama is, then go to that place and convince the world's number one terrorist to stop his holy war and go live in peace and harmony in the Bekka Valley. If he disagrees, kill him but no-one is to know that the Lebanese government is involved. Is that about right?"

How Mac had delivered the synopsis made Norm blanch. It sounded ridiculous even to his own ears.

"Yes," he said weakly, "that's about the gist of it."

The room was silent for thirty seconds or more.

"I was given to understand that rendition camps were in the Eastern block countries, Romania and Poland. Egypt had one too."

"Ah, you have fallen for the great deception. It was inevitable that word would escape about the camps so a deception plan was instigated. The Americans would ensure aircraft landed for re-fuelling at bases in the United Kingdom and Europe. Reporters would be tipped off, then investigate and discover these flights were bound for remote locations in Romania and Poland, as you say. But there are no camps there, the trail is a dead end, look at it from another viewpoint. The Americans have the facility to re-fuel in flight. Why would they have planes land at foreign airports for them to be discovered? Any rendition plane would re-fuel mid-flight and reach its destination without anyone ever knowing about it. The idea is, that once reporters follow the planes that have landed, then write about it in the newspapers, governments can honestly deny that these places do not have camps and that planes landing at airports do not carry prisoners for torture. Even a full investigation in Romania or Poland will show that these camps are being used for storing medical equipment."

"It's very clever." Mac grudgingly conceded.

Who would have thought the Americans would have so efficiently used masquerovka?

Mac referred to the Russian technique of deception, a technique Mac ran his life on.

"Yes, meanwhile the real rendition camps are in Mozambique and Lesotho. Two countries who desperately need foreign aid, especially the American dollar type of foreign aid."

Wow, talk about truth being stranger than fiction. This is political dynamite if ever I've heard it.

Mac took a moment to focus his thoughts as the enormity of the disclosure hit home.

"Is there any event in Zarqawi's life that is personal between them and only Osama and he would know about?"

"I'll look into it and let you know."

Mac gave him a virgin e-mail address.

"Send it there, I don't have time to wait for you. It's seven days to the end of the month. If I don't get the camp's location by following the boat, well, we can't wait another month. Osama's still on the FBI wanted list, his bounty is twenty-five million dollars. I'll want at least that plus expenses."

"What! Twenty-five million! You can not be serious!"

"I can walk out of this room in the next ten seconds and disappear, enjoy my life without interference. If I do not accept this contract you will have failed and your masters will not readily forgive a loss of three billion dollars."

Mac scribbled an account and IBAN transfer number to the First Curacao Bank in the Dutch Antilles, a small island in the Caribbean.

"I'll expect a two million dollar deposit within twenty-four hours, the main deposit of twenty-five million dollars no later than four days from now." Mac's brusque manner had the desired effect.

"I'll see what I can do." Norm rallied.

Mac's demeanour change from brusque to icy cold.

"You want my services, you'll do more than 'see what you can do.'" Mac's words sounded like a voice from the grave.

Norman gulped; despite the coldness he saw in Mac's eyes, he began to sweat.

"Yes, yes, of course."

"Are we done?"

"We... we are done."

"I'll be in touch via the e-mail address you contact me on." Mac left the suite hoping that he could reach the berth before the pain in his head would overcome him.

•••

Henry had spent the last three days in his office, sleeping intermittently on the couch, sustaining himself on coffee and a phlegmy cough.

Helen hadn't seen him like this for over six years.

Not since that horrible episode with Lady Diana Spencer. He really went to town on that one. It affected his health for months afterwards.

All she could do was stay on the couch in her own office and be there when he made the connections. Henry hadn't shaved or brushed his teeth since the last assassination of McDougal; he wasn't sure what had the most roughage, his chin or his teeth. He woke with a start.

"No! It's not possible... is it?"

Quickly moving over to the twin terminal, his hands a blur as images, dates, times, hospital schedules, nurse statements, flashed on the screens.

Could it be? Could it really be as simple as that?

"Helen!" He shouted, forgetting, as the computations whirled through his brain, to use the intercom.

Helen entered quickly, pen and paper at the ready.

"Everything in the fifteen months prior to the 31st August 1997. Every private hospital and clinic in Malta and the South of

France. I need to identify the parents of every child born one year to one month prior to that date. Additionally, I want a breakdown, schedule and diary of every country, city and place that Dodi Fayed visited during the same period. There was a doctor who privately attended the Al-Fayed family, same period for him. Next, Princess Diana, I want a full medical history and diary entries, same period."

Anything else?

"No." Henry answered himself.

Helen had heard Henry answer himself on many occasions, it meant nothing, it was just his assimilation and deductive reasoning in progress.

"Right away, Director." Helen smiled to herself as she turned to leave the office.

He's got the scent, it won't be long before he trees the quarry.

●●●

Ken's meeting with the Ethiopian four days ago had gone very well. They had bartered and eventually agreed a fair price for the Kalashnikovs and grenades.

Ken was now sitting in a thicket on the golf course of Worsley Hotel and Country Club on the outskirts of Manchester, near the tenth hole. A large sand bunker to his right, two small ponds a little further on and an open green fairway everywhere else. The hotel was set in 200 acres of land formally owned by Roger de Worsley and later Geoffrey de Massey, and was eventually bought by Whitbread and developed by Peel Holdings Plc Group in 1984 as a golf course and hotel with conference facilities, gymnasium and indoor pool. In 1995, Whitbread signed an agreement to franchise the rights for the Marriott Group to use its name and manage the hotel.

It was early morning and there hadn't been anyone playing on the green so far. He checked his watch; this time it was a black United States Navy Seal Traser, as used by Special Forces all over the world. Ken had been sitting quietly for nearly three hours, it was no hardship. The wicker basket full of hot vegetable soup, butter laden baps and pork pies did much to keep him alert and fill in the time preparing unusual combinations of sandwiches. Scalding coffee from a military unbreakable flask kept his belly warm and his head clear. He scolded himself at forgetting the Branston pickle to accompany the pork pies and made do with a dollop of liver pâté as recompense.

Oh my. The hardships I endure!

Nearly all the food and drink had been eaten and Ken felt a slight panic at the thought of waiting further without sustenance when he saw what he had been waiting for.

The Ethiopian, who called himself Brigadier-General Mbopo came strolling down the fairway from the ninth hole, dressed in 1940s golfing style with large plus-fours, black and white squared sleeveless jumper and a pair of deep red brogues, the like of which Ken had never seen in his life. The final insult was a flat tweed cap which perched on his head like a plate on a pebble. Brigadier-General Mbopo's caddy was also his bodyguard. Ken had seen him trying to blend in at the bar in the hotel: as inconspicuous as a bishop in a lap-dancing club. He was a large man of obvious strength and carried the bag of clubs with ease, whilst Mbopo sweated with the exertion of walking between holes.

Ken had not chosen the tenth hole simply on a whim. He had chosen it because it had certain advantages but none of those advantages were for either of the two men now walking steadily towards him.

chapter twelve

The Cathedral Peak Hotel stood magnificently amongst the trees exactly as it did in the brochure. Inside Becky wandered around the suite admiring the Zulu masks on the walls, then tried to imitate their grimaces in the mirror.

"What are you doing?" asked Mac.

"Tryin' to make myself look ferocious," Becky replied truthfully, her face contorted into unimaginable shapes.

"Ferocious? They should try and get between you and the Prada concession; believe me, they'd find out what ferocious meant. Right, stop that and come here."

After a final tongue pulling session Becky demurely obeyed.

"It's 9pm now, we'll get something to eat and leave at 5.30am, just as it's getting light. After eating we'll go through the kit then discuss escape routes. If the shit hits the fan, we'll at least have a plan. Any questions?"

"Yeah, do you think they'll have as many choices of mushrooms as the last hotel? They were yummy."

Mac knew she couldn't maintain her focus for too long when she was hungry.

"Right then, little one." He kissed her, fatherly. "Let's see."

Becky closed her eyes as the love they felt for each other washed over her like a warm summer breeze.

She loved him, he knew it.

At 4.00 a.m. Mac lay on the bed; he woke slowly, comfortably, with the thought...

Step three... Infiltration.

By early evening of the same day they had made it to the first tributary of the Orange River.

"This it?" asked Becky hopefully, clothes stained deeply with sweat.

"No, over the next ridgeline, that's the one we want."

Becky had never been in a jungle before, not to mention a grade one canopied jungle like this one. Mac had finished a jungle warfare instructors course in Brunei many years before, knew it was going to be physically tough-going. Becky was being worn down by the heat, humidity, insects and the forty-pound pack on her back. Mac carried almost double that but couldn't let Becky know. Fortunately, Mac anticipated he'd be on the infiltration then route-out within the next seventy-two hours.

It wasn't usual to infiltrate as part of a recce. Normally you would assess the information you'd gathered, plan, source equipment, rehearse then infiltrate. As usual, there just wasn't time to do it by the book.

Aim for the moon, with the expectation of hitting the top of the telegraph poles.

Mac had to do the best he could with the time available; he just hoped that Rashid's heart wouldn't give up under the strain of torture methods that he could only imagine.

Unless you've been there, there's no way you could understand the discomfort, nausea, sweating and disorientation you feel by soldiering in the jungle. Both Mac and Becky were wearing money belts next to their skin which added considerably to their irritation. Inside the belts were $5000 and passports in zip-lock waterproof bags. If everything went to rat-shit and they had to run for their lives the Action On was...

Head east, keep heading east until you came to a township or village. Use the local phone or mobile phone if it has a signal. Call tourist helicopter services, the number is logged under 'contacts', get them to pick you up and take you to the airport in Johannesburg. Ask at any desk for the private terminal, a Leer jet is on standby and will remain on standby for the next seven days. The pilot's name is Isaacs.

Becky slipped... thud. "Shit," she whispered regaining her feet.

"Careful little one, we'll be at the site before nightfall." Mac checked his Silva compass tied to his jacket pocket by para cord.

"We're on track, two hours tops, ok?"

"Ok," she said, wiping her soiled hands on the camouflage trousers and pulling off a leech that was crawling up her pant leg.

•••

Sarah Stewart-Barker had arrived at Hogsleigh Hall two days ago, enjoying a seven day R and R from her duties as a serving Assistant Adjutant in Iraq. As was her custom, fitness rated highly on her schedule and even though she was on leave, saw no reason not to continue her physical training.

Sarah was five-foot eight with long auburn hair and clear hazel eyes. At the moment her chest, a small 'B' cup, seemed much larger as she gulped at the woodland air.

Almost at the top, keep going, keep going.

Although her job in Iraq was essentially administration, at the colonel's discretion she would be allowed on patrol with the men. A position, she knew, that was not easily obtained.

Sarah pushed herself, legs aching, lungs seeming to burst, nearly to the summit of the woodland hilltop four miles from the hall.

Dressed in green military denims, patrol boots and Norwegian top, Sarah made it to the hill's summit, stood, hands on hips, triumphant. Taking large breaths of air, pungent with the smell of ferns and tree musk, Sarah smiled as she checked her army issue watch.

Twenty-six seconds faster than yesterday, tomorrow I'll—
ZING... ZING!

"What the fuck !" Sarah automatically dropped to the ground. Ears alert, calculating the distance between the crack of the rounds going past and the report of sound from the muzzle blast.

Crack and thump is... there is no crack?
Shit. They're using a silencer!

Thwup... thwup

Two more rounds hit the trunk near her head as she searched the woods for the firing position.

They're not large calibre rounds, certainly not the 762 from an AK. Probably not 556 either. Twenty-twos? Yeah, twenty-twos. The rounds were fired too close together for a bolt-action so that means it's a semi-auto. That narrows the range down to under eighty metres.

Sarah rolled, moved location, scanned the woods once again.

There he is, the little shit!

She could see the head and shoulders of a prone figure sighting through a small telescopic sight.

Looks like an AR-7. That's a standard ten round magazine, fired one once. Ok for rats, I aint no rat!

Sarah was indignant.

If I go left I'll be in dead ground to him.

Sarah kept low and pushed herself backwards, turned left and crawled into the ferns. A spider's web hit her in the mouth, she spat it out.

Ugh.

Now in dead ground, she came up into a crouch, picked up speed, heading for a long depression in which ran a small stream.

This'll get me in the direction of home. I'll call the police, find out what all this is about. They'll send up a heli—

Sarah fell to the ground, dead.

Two .22 hollow points hit her in the forehead, she didn't feel any pain, she never would.

"I got her. Come out Jamal," cried a hidden voice.

The first shooter stood up, angry at himself for not hitting her with his first rounds.

"Jamal, you really must get the zero of that scope of yours checked or at least get your eyes tested," Nadeem jibed.

"I only wanted to flush her out in your direction. I know how you need the practice. Come on, it's three miles to the car."

Jamal and Nadeem walked together, both began to disassemble their AR-7s, first taking off the magazine and ejecting chambered rounds, twisting the knurl that held the barrel, pulling it free from the main body then unscrewing the hollow plastic butt from the receiver. Barrel, receiver and magazine all went inside the hollow butt. The shoulder piece pressed firmly into position held all the components secure. Both AR-7s were put into the backpack Jamal carried.

"I really like the countryside," said Jamal. Nadeem frowned incredulously.

•••

"What a shit-hole," said the man sitting in the passenger seat of the battered six-year old Volvo.

"You think so?" He looked around. "I didn't think there was enough of it to merit the compliment of 'shit-hole'."

"What?" he said, slowly getting out of the Volvo. His favourite TV program was 'Sesame Street', he was never going to be a Mensa candidate. His leg ached dully from the two hour drive, the entry and exit holes of where the six-inch nail had penetrated itched like the bite of a thousand ants.

"Never mind. You go speak to the folks in the houses over there and I'll take the houses over here. Meet back at the car in an hour. Ok?"

"Ok boss." he replied glumly, with the feeling he was having the piss taken out of him but unsure how.

"What we after again?"

Don sighed, "We want to know if anyone saw anything suspicious or even a little different on the day of the Prime Minister's assassination. *Anything,* got it?"

"Anything. Got it boss."

Guru limped away in the direction of the houses he'd been allocated. Don spread out a one in fifty thousand scale map on the Volvo roof and began to plot the position of the four mobile phone transponder grid references. Once he'd done that he checked the bearings given in the charts he'd paid a king's ransom for and scribed a line from each of the transponders with his Silva compass.

"Hah!" he exclaimed triumphantly.

The bearings all intersected at one feature on the map.

Looks like a small bridge over the River Tillingham just north of Sowdens Wood. That's where the phones were switched on and where they sent their deadly signal.

They almost got Guru too, poor bastard. One minute a professional soldier in the SAS, the next minute a hobbling civvie. He wouldn't look out of place if he shouted "Mister Dillon, Mister Dillon, the James Boys are in town."

Yeah, and what about me? I'm to take full responsibility as the Commander on the ground for the PM's death. Not one of those smiling monkeys in the civil service so much as lose their salary or get a slap on the wrist. I'm thrown out on my arse with a small pension and not much else. If it wasn't for MI6's Covert Action Cell wanting my services now and again I wouldn't have a pot to piss in. I've got an open invitation to join Tim Spicer's bodyguards in Iraq and maybe I will, at some point, but for now Guru wants revenge and so do I, so we pool our resources. Guru's invalidity award and my pension and off we go. Everyone else is satisfied that the assassin has already been a victim of one of his own bombs but me and Guru, we're professionals, we know better.

Don folded the map and headed in the direction of the houses he'd allocated himself.

Once we've checked these houses we'll head north along the track on the map. It'll bring us out at the bridge. You never know, we may strike it lucky.

●●●

The Brigadier-General was shuffling his bottom from side to side in a vain effort to balance himself for the powerful swing he was about to bring down on the solitary white ball perched on a white plastic tee. His caddy carrier and bodyguard stood behind and to the left of the disco-dancing golfer, his black face split with a wide grin as he watched his master's shenanigans. Slowly the grin changed into a frown and his eyes rolled into his head. He dropped the caddy bag which jangled as it hit the grass and the clubs banged together.

The Brigadier-General whirled viciously.

"Can't you even stay still for a secon..." words failed him and his eyes widened with shock as he took in the scene. His bodyguard lay prone on the ground, he wasn't breathing. Ken, the man with whom only four days previously he had brokered a deal for armaments, was now perched on a shooting stick, dressed like a Vietcong sniper in Tiger stripes. Neat creases ran the length of the trousers and a matching camouflage kerchief was displayed jauntily from his left breast pocket. Ken was relaxed, laconically smoking one of his obnoxious Turkish cigarettes.

It took Mbopo several seconds for his brain to formulate a moderately reasonable response.

"I... what the fuck are you doing here?"

Ken looked around as though Mbopo was talking to someone else in his vicinity. Then, as if it had suddenly dawned on him that he was being spoken to, inhaled deeply, pulled out the defunct cigarette and tapped the long holder on the sole of his boots, before looking directly at the surprised golfer.

"Me? Oh! I'm here to kill you," he said with a devilish smile.

"Kill me? You effete lanky arsehole, how very dare you! You couldn't kill a cold." He laughed, a little hysterically.

"That may be. But you I can handle. However, before I kill you I am instructed to tell you why."

"Go on then, pretty boy. Tell me why anyone would send a woman to do a man's job." He laughed again at his own joke.

Ken was undaunted and unfazed. If anything, he was pleased that the role he portrayed had been so successfully employed. "The guns and grenades you offered me were meant to be sent to the United Kingdom and sold to the various gangs up and down the country. Even though I bought the ones you offered I know you have more and will sell them to people who, shall we say, are not as scrupulous as myself. Even if I refused to buy them, you'd just find someone else and I cannot allow that to happen." Ken remained seated throughout the discussion.

"You can't be serious!" it was slowly dawning on Mbopo that Ken had killed his bodyguard within four metres of him and he hadn't heard a thing and Bwani was no slouch when it came to confrontation. With this thought firmly in his mind he lifted the golf club high above his head and, with a warrior's roar, sped toward Ken with the quickness of a panther.

Ken pulled off the ivory mouthpiece from the cigarette holder which was not brushed steel as everyone thought but solid titanium, a substance much stronger than steel. With the mouthpiece off, it could be seen that the end of the holder was sharpened to a knife-like point. Ken quickly stood and whipped the shooter's stool from behind him throwing it low where it hit Mbopo in the shins and he went down hard with an audible "Umphhh!"

Ken strode forward and turned Mbopo over onto his back where he could look into his eyes.

"I now carry out your summary execution," he said in a voice that was far, far away. Then, without a second's hesitation rammed the sharpened titanium blade up through his ribcage and straight into his heart, ripping open a wide hole by twisting the indestructible blade. Mbopo twitched and coughed red mucus as blood entered his heart and lungs. Checking that the body was without a pulse, Ken wiped the blade on Mbopo's jersey. Picking up the bodies one at a time Ken then rolled them into the nearby pond where they lay in the bulrushes and reeds hidden to the unsuspecting golfers. It wouldn't be too long before the bodies were found, probably by the golf course gardeners, but by then Ken would be long gone. His job done, he walked back to the thicket and collected his wicker basket, backtracked to the public footpath that ran in-between two large houses and out onto the main road where he turned right. Taking the next left, Ken followed signs to the Worsley Garden Centre, where he'd parked the hire car. The garden centre was at the end of the country lane; it had been there for thirty years and was itself a throwback to earlier times, when it was the walled kitchen garden for Worsley Hall and its large estate. There were no security cameras to be seen, which was why it suited Ken's plan admirably. He checked his watch.

If I can make it to the airport before two o'clock I'll be able to make it to Ghana in time to board the cargo ship carrying the arms during its layover period. I'll personally oversee the throwing of those weapons overboard. They'll never be the cause of any deaths here in the UK, or anywhere else for that matter.

On reaching Manchester airport, Ken returned the hire car and registered at the check-in desk, went through to the departure lounge and wandered around until he found what he was looking for. Inserting his fifty-pence coin into the pay-as-you-go internet computer, he opened his email and sent a succinct message saying 'Mission Accomplished.'

Ken didn't have to worry about the cigarette holder setting off the metal detector as he walked through security as he knew that solid titanium did not register as a metal and he could safely take it on board the aircraft without fear of detection or reprisal.

His final thought before he boarded the plane was…

The Director should be pleased with how efficiently this job was handled.

chapter thirteen

An hour and fifty minutes later Mac and Becky sat twenty feet in, under the jungle canopy, away from the Orange River bank.

"Take a break, sit on the bergans." Mac passed her a water bottle. "A little and often, plus never have a drink just before you pee – It goes straight through and you don't get the benefit, ok?"

Becky looked ill but rallied as she took the water. "Ok."

After fifteen minutes of rest, listening to the jungle noises, taking in the environment, Mac got up to move.

"Wait with the kit, switch on your radio. I may be gone an hour or so. I'll check out the river and banking, try and find us a good OP position. Drink more while I'm away, ok, princess?"

Becky wafted straggled hair from her damp face.

"I don't feel like a princess." she murmured.

"Once we've finished here, where do you want to go?"

"Anywhere?"

"Anywhere."

Becky thought hard for a millisecond.

"Milan." Her face brightened considerably.

"Shopping?"

"Yeah shopping, 'n' food, 'n' the beach 'n'..."

"Ok, little one, Milan it is." Even though she was exhausted, Becky brightened.

"Right, I'm off." With that, Mac silently moved into the foliage and disappeared.

Becky sat quietly on the bergan, staring into space.

There's Nina Ricci, Alexander McQueen, Bottega Veneta then I'll try the internet 'n' get addresses of other designers, work out a shopping strategy 'n' street route. I'll need...

After covering two hundred metres Mac found as ideal a spot as he could have wished for. A mound with a depression at its summit that gave 120 degree visibility over the river. They could fasten a low basha over the depression and it would protect them from the worst of the rain. It was also far enough from the riverbank to keep them from the hordes of flies and mosquitoes. He called Becky on the radio: her whispered response came immediately.

"Coming back to your location, be there in twenty. Will call you again just before I get there."

"Roger, out." she said with renewed vigour.

Mac smiled, Becky's motivation had increased tenfold with the mention of Milan.

That's my girl.

Under the basha Mac and Becky took turns on stag. Starting with one hour on, one off, until they had regained their strength. Then, slowly increasing the duration, currently they were doing four on, four off.

During the night time stag Becky had consumed almost three days of rations, cutting off the top and bottom of each tin, squashing the tube flat, inserting the lids in-between the squashed tube sides. Putting the whole thing inside a heavy duty polythene zip-lock bag, just the way he'd told her.

If you don't, we'll be knee deep in ants in a matter of hours. Usually we'd burn any food left in the tins but as we aren't having a fire we can't do that. Keep everything inside containers until we need it.

Becky's clothes were stuck to her with perspiration; she never realised how difficult it was to operate under jungle conditions.

I take my hat off to anyone who can put up with this for longer than a... what's that?

Becky rubbed Mac's shoulder, instantly awake, she moved away slightly as he looked through the spotting scope.

"Where?"

"Ten o'clock, nearside bank, long dark mass moving up river," she said in low tones.

"Seen." Mac re-focused the scope.

"Thar she blows," he whispered theatrically and not a little relieved. Grabbing a prepared black day-pack Mac crawled from under the basha.

"You know the drill, if I'm not back in twelve hours, pack up and go to the hotel. Another twelve then leave, ok?"

"Ok. You'll be alright?"

"I'll be back soon as I know where they're docking." With that Mac jogged up river trying to stay ahead of the battery-powered boat.

Hmph! Not even a goodbye or a quick kiss. Wonder what that fruit salad is like?

Becky opened up Mac's bergan.

Gosh, this is a lot heavier than mine.

It dawned on her what he had done.

"Be safe, my sweetheart," Becky whispered to the rustling trees.

If you're not back in twelve hours, I'm coming after you.

Ten hours later Becky heard Mac's voice over the headset.

"Be there in figures two."

"Roger, out." Becky felt relieved.

Mac suddenly appeared in front of the OP, luck had been with him on several counts. If it had been night when they'd spotted the boat he would never have kept up with it. As it was he had lots of cuts on his face, arms and legs from the spiky flora. He'd seen where the boat had pulled in, spending three hours on a close recce. He didn't like what he'd found, not at all.

The best stroke of luck was that the camp was on their side of the river so they wouldn't have to do a river crossing.

"How'd it go?"

"Good and bad. Eat something and open me a can. I'll have some water too." Mac guzzled thirstily. "We'll both sleep now and I'll give orders for infiltration first thing, ok?"

"Yup. What's the layout like?" Becky's curiosity got the better of her.

"All in good time, little one. Pass me the med kit, I need to treat these cuts before they get infected."

Becky did as she was asked; thirty minutes later they were both soundly asleep.

•••

"Helen, come in please."

The door opened almost before his finger left the intercom button.

"Yes, Director?"

"From 1995 the private physician who attended the Fayed family was Doctor Haidar."

Helen waited patiently for instructions as Henry's gaze focused on a small gouge in the wood panelling on the far wall.

"In June of 1996 he was on the list as a guest speaker at Kings University but I can find no later reference saying what he talked about or even confirmation he actually attended. In addition," Henry waggled his finger at the gouge, "one of the Fayed family's private jets, a Buccaneer, left Stansted on the same evening. What is interesting is that there is no passenger manifest for that flight nor can I find a logged flight plan." Henry paused momentarily. "I have, by process of elimination, worked out from those who were employed as pilots at that time with the Fayeds, where the other pilots were, leaving one pilot and co-pilot unaccounted for."

Helen sat on the sofa; she knew better than to interrupt his mental gymnastics. Many times she had been called in, as now, simply to be a catalyst to his thought process.

"I need verification of: one, did Doctor Haidar attend the meeting. Two, what did he talk about? Three, if he didn't attend where was he and what was he doing? Four, contact the pilot and co-pilot, find out where they flew to, who were the passengers and why all the secrecy?" Henry's gaze focused on the monitor screen.

Helen waited another sixty seconds, stood up, then closed the door quietly behind her, the notepad she carried still blank. It wasn't prudent that she mention "Stork" had sent a Mission Accomplished message. It wasn't vital that he be told now, especially as he was so focused on this other matter.

She sighed, "Just like old times."

●●●

Sitting comfortably in a large bush, Mac checked his watch.
Four minutes twelve seconds.

Becky was around sixty-metres away, at right angles to Mac's location covering his dash out into the open. She'd baulked at Mac's plan, it seemed too risky but Mac had explained in detail; there was no other way.

Mac re-checked his watch, timings were absolutely critical, a second either way could spell disaster, probably death.
One minute twenty-six seconds.

Mac closed his eyes, regulated his breathing. He could hear the birds, the insects, the rustling of the leaves in the humid breeze. As he checked his watch for the last time, his subconscious beavered away, sifting through the audio memories. Slowly he became aware of the fast beat and tune in his head: Paranoid by Black Sabbath. Mac would never realise just how prophetic the words were to become... The loud guitar solo began at zero hour minus six seconds...

At zero hour minus three seconds Becky opened fire with the Blaser paintball gun – Phut... Phut... Phut. A continuous stream of black paint-filled gelatinous balls sped their way to the camera fitted in the tree boughs. The first couple missed, spattering the limbs. Becky corrected her aim, the remaining balls hit home covering the camera lens in their sticky goo. The secondary objective of the splattering noise was to momentarily distract the nearby guard who would look in the camera's direction.

At zero hour Mac came running out of the thicket like an Olympic sprinter; the prize wasn't a gold medal: it was life... his.

Finished with my woman coz she couldn't help me with my life,

Covering the twenty metres of open ground, the only other obstruction was a gully, twelve feet deep and the same wide. Mac took the gully without breaking stride, landed, rolled and continued his momentum toward the guard.

People think I'm insane because I am frowning all the time, All day long I think of things but nothing seems to satisfy,

Becky took an involuntary gasp as she observed the guard begin to turn, some sixth sense alerting him. Mac was still too far away to deal with him.

Think I'll lose my mind if I don't find something to pacify,

Phut… Phut, the paintball gun spat its cargo as the guard saw Mac and lifted his M4 assault rifle in the direction of the approaching figure.

Can you help me? Can't you stroke my brain? Hey yeah.

Phwat, Phwat, two rounds hit the guard in his face; thinking he had been shot for real, he put both hands to his face for a moment believing the goo was blood, the intruder momentarily forgotten. Mac was on him in an instant – Zzzap, the stun gun knocked the guard unconscious. Giving him an extra long pulse ensured he would stay that way for a while.

Becky put the Blaser into her bergan and lay in wait with the suppressed Pietta and three improvised explosives, canisters of black powder each on a three second fuse.

As the tune subsided Mac took hold of the M4, checked the action; it was fully loaded with a curved thirty round magazine. Taking the Sony radio handset from the guard's web harness, he pulled the body to the edge of the gully and rolled him in. The tune stopped.

Phase one complete.

Moving up the slope and out of sight from Becky, Mac moved cautiously. It wouldn't be too long before the Command Post, some hundred metres south, called to check on the guard, maybe asking if a monkey had shit on the camera. Mac had no idea what the guard's voice sounded like, so couldn't do an impersonation.

They've probably got some kinda identification code or trigger word.

On the recce Mac had identified three camera positions. One further down the track near the CP and the other overlooking the cages. As long as he stayed on the slope he'd be in dead ground to it. Still moving stealthily but quickly Mac covered the intervening ground. Taking the Blaser from his back he broke the slope's ridge using a small bush as cover.

Phut, Phut... five rapid rounds splattered the camera lens and its mounting.

Won't be long now before I get a call.

Slinging the Blaser, Mac went forward to the cages – the stench was unimaginable. Six metal cages were slung from a pole about twenty metres long, each cage separated from another by a brick wall that held the supporting pole. The cages were two metres square, suspended a metre or so off the jungle floor. The ground beneath each cage was rancid with the urine and excrement of the caged occupants who were themselves naked.

There isn't time for the subtle approach.

The radio squawked.

"Clint? You there, Clint? What's wrong with the fuckin' camera? Call back."

Mac knew that to delay answering would mean the deployment of a Quick Reaction Force, a team of at least four heavily armed troops, waiting to be deployed.

Mac pressed the pressel switch, then rapidly clicked it off and on several times.

"Wh... I... ca... ok," he said in as casual a manner as he could muster.

In the Command Post the duty signaller called over to the Camp Commander.

"Sir. Clint's got radio problems and cameras two and three are out."

Clint Eastwood was the nickname given to the unconscious guard. Not because he was steely eyed nor because he chewed cigars or was fast with a gun. Clint got his name when on poker nights he would lose with such regularity; he was always asking for 'a few dollars more.'

"Harvey," barked the Commander, "take a handset out to shit for brains will ya?"

"Yes, sir," replied Harvey – anything to break the tedium – he went to the signals store to get one that was fully charged.

Mac knew his radio ruse would bring him only the briefest of relief's. Shaking each cage as he passed, Mac whispered Rashid's name. Four of the cages were occupied. Hundreds of flies and mosquitoes buzzed around the prone figures, too weak to ward off the vicious predators. Bites, stings, lesions and burrowing insects had taken their toll. Mac had visited each cage; no-one responded.

Shit. These guys are in a bad way. Day in, day out, bitten by every kind of insect. Little water, almost no food. I can't even tell one prisoner from another. They're all emaciated, probably dying. This is worse than anything I've been through... The bastards!

Mac changed tack.

Harvey made his way out of the CP.

Becky saw him and took aim. She knew Mac's life was in her hands, no way would she let him down.

"Al-Zarqawi, Al-Zarqawi. I know you are here. Where are you?" Mac asked more urgently this time. "If you don't show me who you are now, I must leave and will never be able to return." Mac listened for a response, precious seconds ticked by.

"He... Here," came a weak voice from the third cage.

"Al-Zarqawi?"

"You know my name. Wh... who are you?"

"Don't talk; listen. Gather all your strength, muster all your reserves. I'm going to shoot off the lock. When I do all hell is going to break loose. Do as I say and hopefully, with Allah's grace, we can all make it home safely. Do you understand?"

"Yes." Then more strongly, "Praise be to Allah." Al-Zarqawi pulled himself into a sitting position; Mac marvelled at his willpower.

Maybe we'll make it after all.

Mac raised the Pietta and blew off the lock. The men in the CP didn't hear the suppressed pistol but Harvey did.

"Harv to base; some—" was as far as he got, the .36 lead ball entered his neck at the artery, hit his spine, ricocheted and exited via his left eye. He crumpled, dead.

Hah! That was a good shot.

"Say again," asked the duty signaller. "Sir, I think there may be a problem. Two and three are still out, no word from Clint, now Harv's not talking."

"Turn out the QRF; go to state Delta, secure the area." Rex barked the orders; he wasn't the Commander for nothing.

The three remaining QRF ran out of the Command Post bunker; as they did Becky laid down her five remaining rounds in an accurate volley, hitting the first guy squarely in the chest; a large red splodge showed on his camo top. The others dodged back into the CP. Throwing the gun into her bergan she lit the first fuse and threw the canister, followed quickly by the other two. Mac's idea was to hit them with everything she had before they had a chance to organise any kind of strategic defence.

Quickly tying the bergan straps she crawled into a dip dragging the pack behind her, staying low as the first of the 5.56 rounds sought her location.

They've reacted quickly, laying down accurate return fire. Mac's not going to get much longer before they storm up to the cages.

While the QRF were shooting at Becky's vacated position, Mac was at right angle to their fire. Half carrying, half pushing the gaunt bedraggled figure, Mac realised they weren't going to get clear fast enough. With the three explosions over, there was nothing else to keep them occupied except the M4 and that would give away his location.

Becky was already at the emergency rendezvous when Mac and a naked guy burst through the foliage. Mac didn't stop; Becky, surprised, felt his urgency and followed. They'd gone about eighty metres when a random volley in their general direction finally burst their bubble of good luck: one round hit Al-Zarqawi, three Becky. Al-Zarqawi suddenly became a dead weight, Mac felt the warm blood oozing over the hand around Al-Zarqawi's back.

"Bex!" Dropping Al-Zarqawi, he knelt over her fallen body and checked her for entry and exit wounds.

A graze on her leg, same on her arm and one into the bergan.

He turned Becky over, pulling off her bergan; the round that had knocked her over hadn't gone through.

"You're one lucky bitch," he said, relief flooding over him, "can you walk?"

"Yeah," she said, her face turning white with adrenaline and shock.

"Go one-hundred metres that way," he pointed, "stop, dress your wounds, look at your watch." Becky did as she was told. "Wait no more than five minutes. If I'm not back, follow the RV procedure, ok?"

Becky nodded, "Ok."

Do what Mac says and everything will be fine.

As Becky limped away Mac turned his attention to Al-Zarqawi. The man was still alive but bleeding profusely. In his weakened state he wouldn't be alive much longer. Bending close to his ears Mac asked urgently, "Where is Osama now? I have a message for him of great importance, you are my only chance of finding him. Please, for the love of Allah help me."

Al-Zarqawi weakly patted Mac's hand, nodded and was rewarded with a convulsion of spitting blood.

"138... 06... 1... 88... 04... 69," he gasped between spasms.

"What does that mean?" Mac looked back in the direction they'd come, the pursuers were getting closer. When he looked back, Al-Zarqawi was dead.

Focus, focus.

Mac was galvanised into action. Dragging the lifeless body in the direction Becky had gone, Al-Zarqawi left a trail a blind man could follow. After thirty metres he left the body, propped the paintball gun on his chest and sprayed the lifeless shell with pepper-spray, then took long strides to 'break track,' ensuring there was no ground trace that he'd changed direction. Looping fifteen metres back in the direction of the patrol, Mac found a good position to spring an immediate ambush. The technique was referred to as 'looping the P.'

If this doesn't work I can always piss on them, I've fuck all left.

Mac was gambling that although these were professional soldiers their concern at capturing the intruders quickly would hinder their awareness and give them tunnel vision; focused so intently, they would be more unaware of their surroundings than usual. Several seconds later the first of the team cautiously arrived and went to the body. Raising a closed hand, telling the others, out of Mac's line-of-sight, to wait, the lead scout scanned the bushes through his Holosight. Mac lay motionless like a dead-fall log. The scout was satisfied there was no-one lying in wait and that the quarry had obviously fled further through the bushes. Spots of blood could be seen ahead on leaves, Becky's blood. It was a safe bet that the quarry had fled down the track after sustaining a hit. Suddenly his nose tingled as the pepper-spray fumes wafted over him but he couldn't let that worry him now that he was so close to the intruders.

The lead scout raised his hand again, two others hurried forward to look at the body and receive quick instructions. The lead scout's eyes began to water with irritation. The two others almost immediately felt the fumes at the back of their throats.

Mac let rip on full auto and, to their credit, the three men from the QRF almost made it. Mac fired twenty rounds then ran forward taking the initiative, it was do or die. The pepper-spray had given Mac that slight edge. None of the team could focus quickly enough through their watering eyes and gain a sight picture with their weapons. Two had been killed outright; the last one, injured, tried to return fire, but Mac emptied the last ten rounds into him. Picking up a fallen M4 Mac threw away his empty one then ran up the track to meet Becky.

"Hi sweetheart," he said as nonchalantly as possible trying desperately to slow his breathing after the adrenalin rush.

Becky had tied military grade field dressings around each graze. It hurt more than it was life-threatening. Mac hadn't told her about the third round hitting the bergan yet, it'd keep.

He checked the dressings, "Good job. We gotta go Princess. Let me help."

As she stood, Mac helped take her weight off the injured leg.

"Where's the other man?"

"Gone."

"You know what this means don't you?"

Mac looked confused.

"At least two days' shopping in Milan." she smirked through the pain.

Mac smiled, he couldn't love her any more if he tried.

• • •

"Anything?"

"Fuck all," answered Guru, his charm radiating like the midday sun.

"I've checked the map co-ordinates and plotted the bearings. If we head north up that track over there, we'll come to the mobile phone initiation site. Looks like a bridge or large culvert over the River Tillingham."

"Any chance of a brew around here?"

Don pulled out the map again.

"Looks like a pub about a click and a half west in Broad Oak, wanna try there?"

"Yeah."

"Ok. But after we check out the bridge, right."

"Sure, Boss, whatever you say." Guru limped around the Volvo.

Don had the sudden urge to say, "Arr, there, Jim lad," but forcefully pushed the sensation away, knowing he would be wasting his breath.

Don put the map away and they trudged the two hundred metres up the muddy track. It wasn't long before they reached the feature Don had described.

"So, it was on this bridge you reckon?"

"Yeah."

"There's fuck all here."

"Yeah, looks like it. Yeah, definitely," he spun round slowly, "fuck all."

BOOM, BOOM.

Don and Guru flung themselves to the floor each reaching for the pistol on their hip that neither now carried.

Don was the first to stand, realising they were not under fire, but something was.

"Over there," he pointed, "sounds like a shotgun, double barrelled by the sound of it."

"Yeah, I thought it was," said Guru getting to his feet and dusting off his clothes.

Sure you did. Hope you're not getting gun-shy, my old friend.

"HOY! You in the bushes," shouted Don, "What's fuckin' goin' on?"

A head appeared over the bushes.

"Me? Oh, sorry bout the noise. Doin' a bit of bird shootin'. Didn't know you were there. Sorry if I scared you," said the floating head belonging to a young local lad.

"You do this a lot?" asked Don.

"On and off. Why? Am I in trouble?" Don ignored the question.

"Were you here on the day the Prime Minister was killed?" Don stabbed in the dark.

"Cor, was I! When I got home it was splashed all over the telly. They even cancelled an episode of Emmerdale. That was my favourite, that was." The boy's voice took on a whining tone.

"Was there anyone on the bridge that day?" Don asked, not daring to hope.

"Cor, yeah. This bird was here."

"Bird?"

"Yeah. Spanish or Italian, something like that. She was wearing a really short skirt, nice pair of pins on her."

"A woman?"

"Naw, not a woman, a girl, fuckin' gorgeous she was. All bent over the wall 'n' all, I couldn't really help myself, took her picture I did. She never even knew I was there."

Don felt sweat on his forehead as he fought to control himself and not kick the shit out of the little pervert.

"You took her picture? How did you do that?" Don asked in as casual and conspirational a tone as he could muster.

"On this." The lad produced a mobile phone from his pocket like a magician's wand.

"Do you still have the photo?"

"Yer. It's one of my favourites," he said with a salacious grin.

"Can I see it?"

"Dunno. It's kinda private you know?"

"Guru?" Guru stepped forward, having heard all the exchange.

"Listen dipshit, you're in a whole heap of trouble. Me and my mate want that phone of yours. Now, you can either hand it over without any fuss or I'll take it from you, savvy?"

The lad started to bring the shotgun to bear on Guru.

"I ain't givin you shit," he said with confidence, smiling at having got the drop on these two misfits.

"It's like this," said Guru conversationally, "that there is a hammerless double-barrelled twelve-gauge shotgun. You fired two shots at the birds and missed and I ain't heard you reload. Have you heard this guy reload Don?"

"Naw."

"So dipshit, do I get the phone or do I take that fuckin' shotgun of yours, ram it up your arse and turn you into a lollipop? What's it gonna be?"

It wasn't so much what he said but how he said it that changed the lad's mind, that, and the murderous look in Guru's eyes.

This isn't a guy I want to tangle with. Fuck it, it's only a phone.

"Ok, no problem, just in the public's interests ain't it... here." The lad handed over the phone, his hand shaking as he did so. Guru took the phone and looked to Don.

"Can I still kick the shit outta him?"

"Naw. Let him go," but then as an afterthought, "we'll have the shotgun though."

"You heard him, gimme." Sheepishly, the lad handed over the shotgun then took off like Linford Christie, throwing a haversack full of 12-gauge rounds onto the road, the red cased ammunition strewn all over the tarmac.

"Leave him," said Don as Guru prepared to give chase. "Get the rounds and we'll go back to the car. Nothing else to be gained from hanging around."

Guru limped up the road; Don shook his head.

"Fancy going to see Pirates of the Caribbean when we've done?" he called after Guru.

"What?"

Don laughed to himself.

"Never mind."

•••

It had been four very busy weeks since the petrol bomb had been thrown through John McBrides window almost killing his precious daughter Rachael. The police had eventually interviewed him but he stuck to the story that he had no idea who may have done it and they left it at that. As there were no clues, there would be no follow up investigation.

Rachael and John had moved into a city centre apartment at 'The Edge.' A large modern apartment block with a concierge and 24 hour security. It was expensive at £1500 per month but that did include all bills, Council Tax and a secure parking space with micro-wave keys that could be deactivated if lost and new one's programmed with a different frequency. The apartment overlooked the River Irwell but then you couldn't have everything.

John didn't try to fool himself; there was little chance of the same thing happening to him here – that really wasn't it. A part of

John was happy that the incident had taken place, not that Rachael had almost been killed, no. He was happy because the actions of the yobs had given him an excuse to be a soldier again. Something that he hadn't quite realised he missed as deeply as he did until that night. He'd convinced himself of the direction he was now headed even though some small part of him felt he had precipitated the yobs actions. The thought left him feeling a little guilty.

The first step in his new direction was research. In the United Kingdom today gun laws were so chaotic and strict that there was little chance he could acquire the equipment he needed using legal channels and it wasn't as if he had any friends or contacts in the criminal underworld. He'd bought a copy of Gun Mart, a magazine devoted to all types of guns, rifles, shotguns and antique weapons. There was also a section on militaria and he perused the advertisements and classifieds with a critical eye. He eventually found some of the equipment he needed, turning to the internet in a Cyber-Cafe on the outskirts of Salford for the outstanding items he required. It didn't take too long and, using several anonymous Yahoo and Hotmail e-mail addresses, contacted them to confirm the items were available.

He was advised that some of the items were out of stock but could be with him in seven to ten days. Next, within the 'business' section of Exchange & Mart magazine he found accommodation addresses and chose one in Middleton Lancashire and contacted them from a pay phone. For £15 per month they would receive letters and parcels, holding them for collection. He typed letters and placed the correct funds in cash in each envelope, posting them on Guaranteed-Next-Day delivery from three different post offices. Within five days the equipment would begin to arrive.

John then turned his attention to a working base. He narrowed his requirements to some kind of lock-up but it must have power and running water. Over two nights he checked the classifieds in the Manchester Evening News eventually finding one advertisement that looked promising. He contacted the company dealing with the rental and arranged a viewing. Sorting out a pair of ripped jeans, checked woollen shirt and working boots from an Oxfam shop, he reckoned he looked like any other rough and ready builder. A woollen hat and two days beard growth completed the ensemble.

He'd finished the initial stages of the operation and now turned to deployment, he needed wheels. After careful consideration and watching for the types of cars used around his area, he selected an 'L' reg E200 Mercedes from a small family run dealership in Stoke-on-Trent. He'd wandered the area until he found somewhere that wasn't covered by street cameras and where cash would be king. He was unaware of the new anti-money laundering regulations that were law in the UK. No single transaction for a vehicle could be paid for with more than £10,000 in cash but as the car John wanted was only £1500 the rules didn't apply. Taking the car on a test drive John was very pleased with its performance. He needed a big car, which the Mercedes certainly was, the only downside was that it had an automatic gearbox but John thought the trade-off was acceptable. Giving the name and address of the mailbox he'd rented, the dealership said they would send the Registration Documents to that address and tax the car for six-months as part of the deal.

John drove the car to a nearby residential area called Penkhull, a quiet area near to the General Hospital. Checking the car was locked and that no-one had seen him from behind their curtains, he left the Merc and went in search of a white van.

By the two week point John had both vehicles stowed away in garages at the same compound he'd rented with the lock-up. The location had been just about perfect with a concrete bunker type building and two asbestos roofed garages all in a three-sided compound surrounded with a ten-foot chain-link fence and a factory wall. He'd walked around the area and had spotted several scenarios that involved shifty-looking men and trucks. He got the impression that if he minded his own business they'd mind theirs.

After a purchasing spree at B&Q and Homebase, John had acquired every piece of machinery and tool that he thought he needed. He checked his bank balance that morning and found less than ten-thousand of his golden handshake remaining.

If I don't watch out money could be a problem. It's not like the army, here I've got to fund everything myself. Fuck it! Sometimes you've just got to grab your balls and jump.

John was no engineer, he didn't have the expertise or experience to operate a lathe or other heavy machinery but he could use a vertical drill and the usual compliment of files, saws and vices. He'd done well on his Battlefield Survival courses and had been singled out to be trained as an instructor in improvised weapons. All this was in addition to the fountain of knowledge he'd gleaned from his paladin press books on silencers, the re-loading of ammunition and many other skills.

He'd picked up the goods he'd ordered via Gun Mart and the internet stores from his Middleton mailbox. He'd phoned beforehand to tell them he was sending a courier to pick it all up; then went himself wearing a leather biker jacket and motorcycle helmet, they had no chance of identifying him.

John was now at the compound bunker setting up the engineering equipment and opening all the other parcels. There were three Walther P99 nine-millimetre blank-fire pistols. These were replicas of the same pistol that James Bond used in his modern tales of daring-do, after he'd upgraded from a Walther PPK in 7.65 millimetre, which was considered a weak round for his type of work. These blank-firers couldn't be bought in the UK but were freely available in most other European countries, these he'd purchased from Spain. There was a Lee re-loading press with a nine-millimetre die and de-capper. Various ammunition cases and bullet heads. Two one litre containers of Alliant smokeless gunpowder, five-thousand small pistol primers and over a dozen other odds and ends. None of the items he'd already purchased required any kind of license except for the gunpowder and that wasn't a license to purchase but a license to store. He'd got around this by saying he was going to use it all immediately so the criteria didn't apply to him. To be on the safe side he'd purchased the powder, heads, cases and primers from different sources and he reckoned it would be some time before he needed to re-order.

I could really kick myself. Twenty-years in the army and I never took a thing. Shit! I could have really kitted myself out.

After bolting the press to the bench, John pulled out the first of the Walther's. It was intent to change it from a blank-firer to a real gun. Admittedly they were made of soft die-cast metal which would fracture under the pressures of firing a normal nine-millimetre round but John was hoping to be able to keep the pressures lower than normal and even the majority of that force would be contained in a new steel barrel, which he would drill out and fix somehow to the Walther's frame. To make matters even more difficult, die-cast metal could not be welded too but John decided it wasn't going to be an issue, as he couldn't weld anyway.

chapter fourteen

She was beautiful, petite and totally absorbed in the magazine she was reading as the 9.15 from Birmingham to Paddington arrived at platform two. The twenty-something male sitting opposite had wanted to engage her in conversation from the moment she'd boarded. He'd eventually plucked up the courage but found, when she pulled out 'Combat,' a martial arts magazine, that the unapproachable aura she radiated became impenetrable and he faltered. In the end he settled for a bacon sandwich and a bottle of Coke from the buffet carriage, probably the wisest decision he ever made.

Natalie Van Reissen, five-foot two and twenty-three years old was a professional killer, a job she had been engaged in since her eighteenth birthday. It wasn't exactly what she had thought of at her career interview in the sixth form of East Ward Secondary Modern but fate had given her a helping hand, in fact it had given her two very fast, very deadly hands.

From the age of four Natalie had been a spectator at her father's dojo where he taught Jujitsu for as long as she could remember. Jujitsu was a very effective form of combat, specifically tailored for use by the Japanese samurai warrior class. By her seventh birthday Natalie was taking part in the classes. By her fourteenth, she was instructing students twice her age and as her fame spread, students would travel from all parts of the country to be trained by her, fight her and, usually, be bested by her. For her sixteenth birthday her father, by working double shifts on the taxi rank, paid for an all expenses trip to Japan to be trained by the Grand-Master himself, who quickly took to Natalie as though she were his own daughter. What should have been a two-week holiday turned into a year-long training session. In addition to mastering the arts of jujitsu and akijitsu she was taught the closely guarded secret art of atemi. A much misunderstood form of fighting known only to a few dedicated Masters, all of them Japanese, save Natalie. Atemi was originally a form of judo taught at the highest level. Instead of the throws for which judo is well known, atemi was the knowledge of devastating blows to parts of the body, nerve endings, arteries and the interruption of the flow of the body's energy known as 'chi.'

Two days after her eighteenth birthday Natalie found herself at the World Martial Arts Championships in Tampa, Florida. The championships ran over four days and brought entries from all over the world. Students came to fight each other in 'semi-contact' events and to be judged on their 'kata,' a series of structured and rigorous moves that must be choreographed and performed perfectly.

Natalie fought well in each bout, slowly progressing thorough the knock-out stages and eventually to the final. As she stood in her corner waiting to be called forward and face her opponent from the Netherlands, she felt a warm wave of calm over her face, something she had heard about from her Sensei's who had described it as the warrior's mindset, a feeling of being prepared to die, embracing that thought and, by way of acceptance, freeing your mind and body of all doubt and consequence. By accepting your willingness to die, you invariably didn't, which was something of a paradox. As far as Natalie was concerned it was no longer a fair contest; she knew, without uncertainty, that she would defeat her opponent. And she did.

Throughout the heats Natalie had noticed a tall, well-built man of about her own age watching her from the spectator stands. She was quite naive about matters of sexuality and had little experience of men and their ways. She'd had the usual fumbles with boys at the rear of the school bikeshed but nothing more. With all the training she did there wasn't much energy left for anything else and Dad was always around. The students that came to the dojo had too much respect for her father to ask her out. Well, respect and not a little fear.

Carrying the winner's trophy back to the dressing room the man she'd noticed watching her came forward and shook her hand.

"Hi. My name's Toby. You looked really great out there. I've never seen anyone execute such a perfect manoeuvre. What was it called?"

"Osoto-gari, major-outer-reaping-throw."

"Well, your Osoto whatsit was very impressive but not nearly so impressive as you are close up. Any chance we could meet up later for a drink or something?"

He's gorgeous. Not too tall. Great body, nice smile. Why not?

"Sure. I'll meet you at the entrance once I'm showered and changed." She beamed, flattered that someone would be interested in her. Natalie's mind was already searching for the excuse she would give her father for slipping away.

• • •

The reception area of the surgery waiting area was the cleanest and most orderly he'd ever seen. From the rich oak panels of the lobby walls to the eighteenth-century chandelier that hung magnificently from the ten-foot wide ceiling rose. As a keen, albeit amateur, historian Detective Sergeant Richard George felt quite awestruck at the organised splendour.

DS George felt compelled to run his fingers over the early eighteenth-century Austrian cupboards. The fine inlay and marquetry had stood the test of time; it was a rare example and obviously cost a fortune.

More than I make in ten years, easy.

DS George, 'Ricky' to his friends, was an old-school policeman. He was a bear of a man and shambled along as though all the worlds responsibility was on his shoulders. With shoulders the size of his, he could probably take it. At six-foot six and coming almost to the end of his police career, there wasn't much that he hadn't seen. Man's inhumanity to man had ceased to amaze him several years ago. Dressed like a fifties throwback in a hat, raincoat and Dents black leather gloves, he radiated both weariness and confidence at the same time. Ricky always thought he'd been born a little too late and could see himself as the tough but fair detective in a Mickey Spillane thriller.

He caught the eye of the female receptionist whose visage would not look out of place on the cover of Vogue and padded over to her.

"May I help you, sir?" she asked with enough sugar in her voice to make a spoon stand up in a mug of police canteen tea. It was immediately obvious that she thought he had wandered in off the street and was lost, here to ask directions, or something similar.

"Actually yes, there is something you can help me with. I'm here to see Doctor Haidar." Ricky tried a charming smile but the gaps in his teeth made them look like lonely icebergs and did nothing but grant him a withering acknowledgement.

"Do you have an appointment?" she asked, already knowing that he didn't.

"Yes," he answered still smiling, "here it is." He produced his warrant card and held it steadily level with her face which almost turned pink. Maybe it was his imagination.

The receptionist looked down at the telephone system, pressed several buttons and waited; it was answered in an instant. She gave a succinct explanation then replaced he receiver.

"The doctor can give you ten minutes," she said haughtily, trying to regain the pecking order. Ricky grunted and followed the direction of her pointing hand.

"Room two." If Ricky had brought a beer he could have chilled it with the tone of her voice.

Ricky wandered down the long hallway. Half-way down, there was a flower arrangement that he knew for sure was worth more than his week's salary.

"I must be in the wrong business," he muttered under his breath.

It wasn't long before he came to room two, he knocked and heard the commanding word, "Enter."

Sounds like a man used to being obeyed.

Ricky opened the door and almost blasphemed at the opulent interior. The room was of a manor house in its proportions, high ceilings with original ornate coving. The walls had both a chair rail and a picture rail harking back to earlier times. On the walls were pictures of horses, a landscape and someone who looked like a well-to-do earl resplendent in the garb of a chasseur and with a handlebar moustache the length of Cornwall.

At the far end of the room was a large dark wood desk adorned with the usual objects: lamp, blotting mat, pens, phone. Except all were of a very expensive quality.

Doctor Haidar rose from the deep brown leather chair and held his hand out. Ricky took it and shook it vigorously; the strength in Ricky's hand was not returned.

"So, what is it that I can do for Metropolitan's finest?"

Ricky wasn't sure if the doctor was taking the piss or not. The doctor's open expression convinced Ricky he was on the level and he let it pass.

"Well, sir. We're looking into our outstanding cases. Nothing for you to worry about, I'm not here to arrest you. It's just, you might be able to help us with our enquiries."

"In what way? Please, sit." Haidar offered the detective a seat, which he promptly took.

Ricky opened his notebook. It was for effect, as he knew the contents by heart.

"In June of 1996, you attended a meeting as guest speaker at King's University; is that correct?"

The change in Doctor Haidar's demeanour was instantaneous, he was not a man used to lying and the directness of the question hadn't allowed him to think fast enough.

"Err... yes... I... I... of course... I..."

"Doctor. I want you to think about the nonsense of what you've just said. Take a moment to reflect and consider what will happen if I report back to my superiors that I don't believe you know anything. First, I am not a regular policeman but report back directly to Special Branch," he said, lying his arse off. "Second, the people that I work for will have you struck off in an instant. All this," Ricky waved his hands at the surroundings, "will be but a distant memory. In addition, I have no doubt that within forty-eight hours of me leaving your office there will be over two-hundred child pornography pictures which will materialise on the hard-drive of your computer. Am I making myself clear?"

Doctor Haidar didn't know what had hit him; in other circumstances he'd found that blustering served him well but knew it would be futile with this man. He considered his position, his friends, the current social life he and his wife enjoyed. He studied the man sitting in front of him and came to the conclusion, wrongly, that he wasn't bluffing.

Hesitantly the doctor wiped his sweating forehead with a monogrammed silk handkerchief, considered his options, then began to talk quietly behind steepled fingers.

●●●

Let's hope it doesn't blow up on me again.

It was late afternoon and John McBride was deep in the bowels of Ashworth Valley, classed as an area of outstanding natural beauty between Bury and Heywood. John wasn't sure if it was still within the area now known as Greater Manchester or not. He was here, not to admire the scenery, but to test the latest incarnation in his quest to turn a blank-fire replica into a real semi-automatic pistol. This was his sixth attempt, the last time it exploded and had he not put his leather gloved hand around the other side of a tree stump when he fired; the blast would have thrown shrapnel into his face and injured him quite severely.

So far I've had feed problems, ejection problems, magazine alignment problems, every other fuckin' problem you can think of but now, now I think I've got it. last time; the charge in the round was way too high but I've dropped it from 3.5 grains to 2.8. that should still give me at least 900 feet per second but if this works out then I'll try a series of penetration exercises, see how that goes. Ok, let's see if I can blow myself up today.

John selected a large Dutch elm and positioned himself behind it. Pulling the top slide back he chambered a .380 cartridge that he loaded with Alliant powder.

No problems with the chambering. It slid nicely up the feed ramp and engaged with a solid thump.

It was a 95 grain FMJ bullet head and he hoped that when he pulled the trigger it would fire, eject the spent cartridge and load a fresh one from the magazine. He'd started with NATO standard nine-millimetre cases but at nineteen-millimetres long; the case wouldn't seat or feed properly into the chambers mouth add that it was too tight in the magazine; causing stoppages and eventually John had to discard that idea. After much consideration John had tried a .380 case which; at seventeen-millimetres long allowed the bullet head to be seated further down the case for an overall length of just under twenty-three millimetres, the same length as a nine-mill blank. One final check that a round had in fact been chambered, he placed the Walther on the opposite side of the tree and pulled the trigger.

BLAM!

John tentatively brought the gun from round the tree and pulled back the top slide an eighth of an inch to see if it had loaded a new round.

"Fuck me." he exclaimed. "It did it."

John ejected the magazine and cleared the round from the breech. Once the gun was safe he striped it down to its major components and closely inspected the parts he'd added for stress fractures or movement.

It's fuckin' rock solid.

As a final point he inspected the barrel just in case the bullet had lodged inside because of insufficient power. It was clear.

Right, that's one round. Let's see what it's like after another five.

He took his position again and fired off the remaining five rounds in quick succession.

BLAM BLAM BLAM BLAM BLAM!

He went through the same routine as before, still; there was no sign of fractures or movement.

Great! I only ever expect to fire twenty or thirty rounds through these then I'll throw them away and make new ones. Now, all I have to do is put a thread on the end of the barrel, make a competent silencer, line up ten baffles with a hole in their centre with only a quarter of a millimetre either side for the bullet to go through and with sufficient solidity to withstand a the pressure of a round travelling at nearly supersonic velocity... piece of piss.

Checking there was no-one in his immediate area, John placed the Walther in a Marks and Spencer's carrier bag then put it in his day-sack. It was a mile, up the zig-zag path that wound its way along the valley wall to where he'd left his car.

•••

Mac stood under the canopy of intertwined palm leaves, looking out over the thunderous waves of the Pacific Ocean.

Becky was still uppermost in his thoughts and he fought to reconcile his concerns for her and focus on the immediate job at hand. He loved Becky, what's more, he knew it. Her being shot and the possibility that he could lose her that way had shaken him terribly. So much so, that he felt he could no longer put Becky in the line of fire and had written to her explaining that she would be better off living a normal life without him, and the dangerous situations in which they found themselves. He'd rather live without her, knowing she was safe, rather than with her and in danger. It had been the hardest letter to write in his entire life. He nearly didn't finish it.

Focus, focus, focus. Push it away. Remember your training.

It was early May, the start of a rainy season that would last for four months. Dark grey clouds unleashed their cargo of warm rain. Mac stepped forward, tilted his head upward feeling the sting of the downpour. He raised his hands outward as if to catch the life-giving droplets. He laughed at himself, a warm, vibrant infectious laugh.

The two young native Salvadorian waitresses watched, incredulous at the antics of the 'gringo,' but they understood too. The rain had a cleansing effect on the land, cities and villages. Whatever had been troubling the man had been washed away also.

After five minutes Mac lowered his hands, turned and went back under the shelter of the palm roof. In his drenched clothing he sat in one of the cheap white plastic chairs at a cheap white plastic table. He smiled at Lorena and Maybelle, they flashed pearl-white in open innocent return.

"Café, por favor."

"Si."

Lorena scurried away to the kitchen area, returning with a silver jug of warm weak coffee.

"Gracias." Mac sipped the brew appreciatively, holding the small cup in both hands.

Lorena and Maybelle stood about twenty-feet away, both dressed in the Tesoro Beach Hotel's standard black trousers and dark-blue blouson-style top, each slender girl with her jet black hair pulled back into a pony tail. They regarded Mac as someone who was troubled. Even if they spoke English they would have thought it bad manners to ask what ailed him. Whatever it was now seemed to have been resolved and they were instinctively pleased for him.

Mac placed the cup on the chipped Korean saucer and reviewed his position.

Right! Before he died, Al-Zarqawi gave me a set of numbers as to where he'd been told to go to if he ever received a recall message. He believed that the numbers gave the location of Mister Bin Laden, he couldn't see any other reason for their use. The numbers were latitude and longitude, minutes and seconds. Accessing the internet and searching on Google I found that the co-ordinates came to a mountainous area in El Salvador, Central America, near the Honduran border. Becky has used up her nine lives. On the hot extraction she'd taken three rounds, one had hit the bergan she was carrying and been stopped by the equipment and Kevlar vest I'd cut in two, putting half in each of our packs. One round had nicked her arm and the other her leg.

Mac paused and took a deep breath at the memory then continued.

She's in the UK recuperating and I've come to El Salvador in the hope of finding Bin Laden's lair. If he is here, it's a stroke of pure genius, who would think of looking for him in Central America?

Recalling the events helped sharpen his focus.

I need a local map of the area, transport, food, water, bergan etcetera, etcetera. This place should be crawling with surplus guns. I ought to be able to pick something up from somewhere.

Mac took another sip of the coffee.

The information I downloaded and read on the flight said that there was quite a criminal element here. As well as the usual street crime there were the organised gangs, most notably the 'Mara' gangs. Last year 1800 gang members were killed by other gangs and a further 300 were killed by Government forces.

It advised against wearing jewellery, watches or even designer clothes. Kids as young as eleven would carry out armed robbery just to take your mobile phone. Handguns, .22 rifles and pump-action shotguns could be bought from registered gun dealers but only by Salvadorians with a national identity card and then only after a seven day waiting period so you could be checked out for a criminal history.

I'll try the direct approach first, see how that goes.

Mac stood up, only now realising how wet he was. The two girls watched as he headed to the reception area and the corridor that lead to his room.

"He seems so sad; so..."

"Alone?" Added Lorena.

"Yes, alone," continued Maybelle.

"But he had a nice pert bottom... for a gringo."

"Yes, for a gringo; it was very nice."

The two girls giggled together looking around to see if any of the management had overheard.

The gringo was the only customer at Tesoro Beach, the tourist season had finished a week ago and the resort was really only open for repairs and essential maintenance. But, as Mac arrived and paid $3000 cash for a fourteen day all-inclusive stay, the manager hadn't seen a problem with it.

There were one hundred and twenty chalets in two rows. Mac was in number 1226 at the very end of the corridor on the ground floor. He had his own fifteen-foot long 'dipping' pool. It was 10.12am and already twenty-eight degrees. Mac looked through the patio windows and up into the sky.

Clouds are clearing already, by lunchtime it'll be up around thirty-four degrees.

He stripped and showered in the tepid water, his skin still laced with the criss-cross scratches from thorns and leaves as he and Becky had run through the jungle, trying to keep ahead of the team they knew would have no hesitation in killing them. The Americans would never want the secret location of their rendition program revealed.

Mac knew only the very basics of the country's native language: Spanish. Fortunately the young receptionist called Danny had spent three years in the United States before the Immigration and Naturalisation Services caught up with him and he was deported.

Danny had answered any question put to him; he was completely without guile and eager to help.

Mac confirmed the location of three gun shops in San Miguel, about a two hour drive north-east of Tesoro Beach. A yellow taxi had been ordered and a fare of fifty dollars, one way, had been agreed.

Always best to agree a price first. That way they won't try an' rip you off. Well, not as much as they'd want to.

As the taxi made its way through the countryside on well-tended roads, it became evident just how big the gap was between the 'have's' and the 'have-nots.' Corrugated tin shacks, bin bags for a roof, woven palm fronds for a fence. No electricity or clean running water. You couldn't drink the water from the taps at the hotel.

So what chance do these people have?

Mac noticed that even though they lived in appalling conditions, almost everyone he saw was clean and tidy. Especially the schoolchildren, whose uniforms were parade-ground immaculate.

It says a lot about the people.

It hasn't exactly been a country high in the 'luck' stakes. Twelve years of civil war, finishing in '98. Then Hurricane Mitch which destroyed almost half the houses and production plants.

Then the earthquake centred around San Vincent just three years later.

The government's corrupt, along with the majority of the police force. Presidente Saca is under Bush's thumb and eighty-five percent of the country is owned by two percent of the population.

If you're born in one of these shacks, the only way out is crime, robbery or drug exportation. You can't sell drugs in El Salvador as the average wage is six dollars a day or less.

The two-hour drive went by quickly and there was only one flash downpour the whole journey.

As they entered the outskirts of San Miguel, Mac saw that many stores had private security guards dressed in green uniforms, each with a white embroidered number over their left breast pocket. They all carried a very large, very intimidating pump-action shotgun.

You don't have to be an expert to pull the trigger on a shotgun. Even if you point it in the general direction of the enemy you're gonna hit something.

Traffic was slow and Mac took time to get the feel of the place. He noticed there seemed to be a lot more women than men. Danny had mentioned that the ratio was five to one but Mac had thought he was exaggerating; now he wasn't so sure.

•••

"This the place?"

"Yeah. According to the licence plate we got from the photo out of the perv's phone, this place rented the car out."

"We were lucky on that, weren't we."

"Fuckin' right, about time we had a run of good luck," said Don.

"How we playin' it here?"

"You stay outside, stop anyone from coming in. I'll talk to whoever's inside and try to charm the information out of them."

"Ok, Boss; no problem."

Don opened the door to the Hertz shack and spoke to the young girl on duty.

"Hi. Do you do Range Rovers?"

"Yes, sir. You'll need a driving licence, a household bill and two different credit cards." she said with a business smile.

"Oh, gosh," said Don in his best plummy accent.

"I only have one credit card with me. Can you tell me if you have a Rover available for the end of the month?"

The girl checked her monitor and the paint on her nails at the same time.

"Yes sir, we could arrange that. How long for?"

"A week. Tell you what. I'll go and get my other credit card and come back. How's that sound?" he smiled. A perfect row of teeth glistened in the overhead lights and almost dazzled her. The young impressionable girl couldn't help but reciprocate.

"Thanks for your help. See you later." Don exited into the street.

Guru watched as Don crossed the road and went into Lindy's Cafe.

"Two teas please, love."

Guru wasn't far behind Don and sat in a window seat waiting for his cuppa.

"So what's the score, Boss?" he asked eagerly.

Don plonked the two teas down on the plastic tablecloth with a Union Jack design.

"Result. We got her address."

"Yeah? Fuckin' great." Guru smiled malevolently and took a noisy slurp of the hot brew.

No way was Don going to tell Guru that he'd got the address yesterday from his friend Chris at MI6 HQ. Guru wasn't to know that he'd been recruited into the Increment, an ad hoc unit used for covert deniable ops. Guru would only be jealous and resentful if he found out and Don needed him. He'd come in useful for back-up but Don wanted him as more of a 'patsy' if things went wrong.

I've been a fall guy once and didn't like it. We no longer have official sanction and if things get out of hand, well, he's a mate and all that, but if it comes down to it, Guru can take the heat.

•••

The best gun shop was on the first floor over a sports store and shoe shop. The ever-present security guard on the walkway took obvious pride in his work. Not dressed in the usual green garb Mac had seen previously but in black from head to toe, a black assault vest with fifty or more blue plastic 12-gauge shells for the Mossberg pump-action shotgun that hung loosely from his shoulder. The guard smiled a toothless welcome and opened the door to the premises. Inside was not as well stocked as he would have liked but it had been recommended as being the largest of the three. On the left were odds and ends of magazines and holsters. In front was a selection of revolvers, .38s, .38 specials and .357s. Half right were automatic pistols, 9 mil Steyrs, a large civilian model, a couple of older Sig-Sauer P225's and a small silver .380 auto. On the far right wall were .22 semi-auto rifles and half a dozen air-rifles. The shop was serviced by two women, one of whom came forward and spoke to Mac in Spanish.

Mac shrugged, pointed to the Steyr then to his eyes, the girl caught on and pulled out the pistol from inside the glass cabinet. The price tag said fifteen-hundred dollars; it wasn't the price that bothered him, it was not having the right ID.

Mac pressed the release and ejected the magazine, checked there were no rounds in either the magazine or chamber then fired off the action in a safe direction. The other woman who had witnessed Mac checking the action came from behind the rear desk.

"May I help you, Señor?" She said in heavily accented English.

Mac took in the traditional shawl, hair tightly pulled back into a chignon, laughter lines on her oval face and thick sensual red lips; her eyes were bright, intelligent and curious.

"Depends, Señora. I may have a proposition for you, is there somewhere more private we can talk?"

Carmen took in the man's build.

Like a dancer, or maybe even a cat. His competence and familiarity with the Steyr indicates a man who has used such weapons before. But more than anything it is the look in his eyes, darkness, sadness, a deep weariness. I have seen such a look once before.

Carmen had once been married to a military man who fought and died in the civil war. She loved him completely, with a passion and ferocity she never knew she had in her; she missed him still. Carmen hesitated for just a second.

"Please Signor, follow me."

Mac went round the cabinet, passed the astonished assistant and through the only other door into a rear office.

The woman was in her early forties and had kept her figure well.

Kelly Brook, eat your heart out.

She and her husband never had children, a fact she regretted almost every day. Taking her place behind the deep rosewood desk, she raised her hand in greeting.

"Carmen Maria de la Spirosa," she said quickly.

"Robert Maxwell de London," Mac replied with a beatific smile.

Well, if I'm gonna con the woman I might as well have the right name.

"I'm sure it is not, but that does not matter here, does it?" Carmen returned the smile sincerely. "You said you had a proposition for me?" Her left eyebrow raised slightly. Mac could see the humorous glint in her eyes.

"Yes." Mac heard also the playful note in her voice.

"I was thinking that maybe the business I had in mind could be conducted on this desktop," he paused, "but if you think that may be too… uncomfortable, we could continue on the floor." Mac theatrically pressed his foot into the carpet. "It seems like it could take it."

Carmen flushed, slightly unsure now; she rallied, countered.

"Do you think this… business will be over quickly or do you think it will… last?" She stared hard into Mac's eyes, holding his gaze.

"It will last as long as you want it to, or over quickly and then I'll be gone... the choice is entirely yours." The room was sexually charged; Carmen had not felt this way for many years.

A stranger walks into my shop and within minutes we're in the back room speaking innuendo and double-entendre, when all I really want is to have him inside me right here, right now. What must I be thinking?

Mac had, up to this point, thought this exchange had been fun, a way of introducing a little light-heartedness into what could be a dangerous discussion. Suddenly aware of her dilated pupils, slightly swollen lips and heart-felt gaze, his usual state of situation awareness momentarily deserted him; this was not at all what he had anticipated.

It's time to bring matters to a close.

"Shall I pull it out and put it on the table so you can see it?" he smirked.

"Si, I would like that very much," she replied breathlessly.

Mac put his hands into his pockets and pulled out two rolls each of ten-thousand dollars. Carmen's eyes widened at the sight of the money and the realisation that this gringo's words had not held the meaning for which she had hoped. Her cheeks blushed a deep pink and she sat down quickly into the leather seat.

"For what do you want with this?" Carmen asked testily, recovering and rubbing her sweaty palms along the seam of her skirt, pointing then to the dollar bills.

"You're right; my name is not Robert Maxwell and you're also right that it does not matter. I need a high magazine capacity semi-auto pistol, three spare mags. A twelve-gauge pump-action shotgun, preferably with a magazine extension. I need a hundred rounds for the pistol and thirty rounds for the shotgun. I have no identity documents and I am not a Salvadorian citizen. If you can help; the twenty-thousand is yours."

Carmen looked at Mac from the matching rosewood armed chair as the real reason the gringo wanted to speak with her became evident.

"I can pick up the telephone and have the Policia National Civil here in less than a minute."

"Or," said Mac quickly, "you could shout out and have the store guard come in and shoot me for being a menace."

"Yes, I could," she agreed smiling, regaining some composure.

"Or, you could simply keep the money and give me what I want," Mac said hopefully. He didn't want to have to kill the guard even though it would give him the shotgun he needed. Carmen earnestly studied Mac's face.

This is not the face of a criminal, a terrorist or even of a bad man. While I can see the darkness in his eyes, it is not in his soul. The store could really do with the money but....

Carmen continued to study Mac's face, then stood; a decision had been made.

"Wait here, Señor, I will be but a moment." With that, she quickly made it to the door and closed it behind her. Mac decided that two minutes should qualify as 'but a moment;' after that he was gone. Twenty seconds before his deadline she reappeared carrying a large brown leather suitcase. Carmen seemed fit but she was struggling with its weight. Mac took it off her and heaved it onto the desk top. Carmen went back to the door and pushed the bolt across so they would not be disturbed. Taking hold of the case she depressed the unlocked studs and the spring hinges flew open.

"Everything in my store is registered with the Policia. These were my husband's from the war and have never been registered."

Carmen opened the lid and showed Mac the contents. There was a bandolier of 12-gauge rounds, some with markings on them to show they contained ten ball bearings; deadly in a jungle environment. There were six shells with the inscription 'Dragons Breath' and four with 'Bolo' inscribed down the shell length. Mac knew of these but had never used them and was surprised to find them in Central America.

Next was a twenty-inch long six-shot cut-down Remington 870 shotgun, one of the most enduring and competent shotguns ever produced. Mac checked the pump-action.

"Sweet," he said, meaning every word.

"Everything is as my husband left it. No doubt it is well-oiled and in good working order."

At the bottom of the case, below a set of camouflage trousers were a pair of Tokarevs in matching holsters. Two pouches, each carrying two magazines, were fixed to the matching web belt. Before checking the pistols, something else caught his eye. On the belt was an unusually slim knife scabbard with a round handle protruding from the top. Mac pulled it clear.

Wow! An original D-Day cruciform knife. I've seen them in books but never in reality.

The blade and handle were forged from the same piece of steel. The handle was about four-inches of turned steel and chequered to help with grip. There was no crossguard or quillion, the handle just stopped and the tapered cruciform blade began. Each of the four cruciform blades were sharp but not overly so, tapering very gradually to a rapier point. This was primarily a stabbing weapon, in its day, produced in thousands for the D-Day landing in June 1944. Once the enemy was stabbed, even if they were not immediately killed, the wound made by the cruciform blade would look like an 'x' in the skin. This would keep the wound open and they were likely to bleed to death anyway.

"Where did your husband get this knife?"

"Someone, an old army friend, sent it to him from America. You like this?"

Mac held the knife infront of his face, slowly turning the knife, committing each facet and edge to memory.

"It's beautiful."

Men and their toys.

The two Russian TT-33 Tokarev pistols were in excellent condition. Using the now obsolete 7.62 x 25 round, it was a powerful pistol lacking firepower only from its limited magazine capacity of eight rounds. However, if you got hit by one of these rounds, you stayed hit and were unlikely to ever get up again. They were large heavy pistols on a par with the American Colt.45 from whom they had obviously been copied. After checking both of the actions and ensuring the firing pins weren't bent or damaged, Mac laid the weapons back in the suitcase.

"Are you sure you want me to have these?"

"I am sure. My husband would have wanted his weapons to be used. Lying here in a suitcase would somehow have grieved him."

Mac locked the suitcase clasps.

"I will put them to good use, Señora. You have my word. Please, I know you will refuse but take the money and put it to good use."

Carmen hesitantly accepted the offered funds.

"Gracias. I will."

Mac pulled the suitcase off the desk, whirled, unbolted the door and stepped into the store. Almost at the entrance he hesitated, dropped the case and walked purposefully back to the rear office. Carmen was taken aback as Mac took her into his arms, they kissed passionately. Almost a full minute later Mac released her.

"For luck," he said.

"Si," she looked deeply into his eyes, "for luck."

chapter fifteen

1989

Mac had been leading several teams from Saudi Arabia deep into Iraq. Desert Storm hadn't happened yet and the various international governments had not yet decided Saddam had to go.

As a team leader in the Special Observation Troop, Mac's job was to lead other teams and individuals into Iraq and sometimes to get them back too. Mac's current assignment found him waiting six kilometres from the Saudi – Iraq border in a temporary base camp awaiting the arrival of his 'passenger.' The Jet Ranger helicopter deposited his charge without ceremony and immediately 'dusted' off.

Mac, in desert camo gear, recognised the man straight away. Not that they'd ever met, he just knew the type. The guy was in his mid twenties, wearing brand new out-of-the box camo gear and carried an M16A1 assault rifle. Mac waved and the guy trotted over.

"Hi, I'm…"

"Stop right there. I don't need to know your name; you don't need to know mine. You're Charlie and I'm David, ok?"

"Sure," he held out his hand, Mac shook it and they walked to the mess tent.

Chaz 'n' Dave. What a fuckin' double act.

After reorganising Charlie's equipment and spending some time on patrolling skills, they ate a final meal at 17.30 hours then headed to the briefing room. Charlie was from either MI6 or SIS, Mac guessed. He was no regular soldier, fit enough, but from a gym, not by working on the ground.

Mac had been ordered to baby-sit several such individuals, taking them from the relative safety of Saudi Arabia, over the border into Iraq. Mac would only ever know the part he was playing. Sometimes he would lead a group then leave them to stay, get on with whatever it was they'd been briefed to do. Sometimes they would make their own way back, sometimes they wouldn't and Mac would take command and lead them back to friendly lines. It was simply a case of need-to-know.

At the briefing Mac learned he was to infiltrate with his charge sixty kilometres into Iraq, east of plateau Delta. They were to set up an observation post for five days, photograph everything they saw and exfiltrate back to the border checkpoint. Tentative routes were discussed, arcs of observation laid down. They were expecting a deployment of Scud B 8x8s, intelligence sources had declared modifications to the missile's propulsion system. Now, physical confirmation was required.

After the briefing, Mac took Charlie to one side and went through hand signals, actions on and immediate action drills. They would only be travelling at night, covering a maximum of ten kilometres per night. Mac estimated six days plus two days for any deviation off route.

"It all looks good on paper but there will always be patrols, camps or convoys that we will only know are there once we see them." Mac's voice lowered. "There's only one major rule. Do what I say when I say, don't think about it; just do it, ok?"

Charles swallowed and stammered, "Ok."

They set off at midnight, Mac leading, Charlie ten feet behind. He'd been told to watch Mac's feet and place his in the same spot. Mac scorned small calibre assault rifles like the M16, Famas and Car 15. Mac had always carried a 7.62 x 51 Nato standard self loading rifle, referred to as the SLR. He'd made a few modifications, an extended butt, telescopic sight and folding bipod. The other, but more major, modification was the long suppressor. Mac had made friends with a Saudi Army armourer; between them they designed a takedown suppressor. It was not designed as a 'silencer,' rounds leave the barrel at almost 3000 feet per second, even should a silencer be fitted, the crack as the bullet goes through the sound barrier, could not be eliminated. The 'Reflex' suppressor was only six inches longer than the barrel but extended its whole length, as far as the gas plug. Perforated steel baffles allowed the gases to expand and muffle the explosion. The enemy would have great difficulty in locating the firing position, which was the whole point.

Charlie had remarked on Mac's 'cannon.'

"Out there it's a desert and mountains. What you've got is fine for the jungle but here? I don't aim to get that close. With this," Mac held up the SLR, "I can keep their heads down at over 800 metres, at 600 I can hit those same heads. And, with its knockdown power it's not so bad at close quarters either. When the shit hits the fan, you'll empty that magazine of yours in three seconds, most of it going high with the full-automatic recoil. I'll have fired two rounds. You'll have hit fuck all and I'll have two dead enemy, ok?"

Charlie felt he'd been educated and chastised at the same time. "Ok."

Mac stepped up the pace over the first three days; Charlie remarked on it.

"While we're still near our own lines and there's a problem we can still go back. As we get closer to the objective we can slow down and use any time we've previously saved, take things a bit slower. You'll find we've been doing about three 'k's a night over the last few nights, ok?"

Charlie nodded, it made sense. "Ok."

On the fourth night they came upon an unexpected obstacle.

"Minefield," whispered Mac. "It'll take too long to go round and even then there will be patrols at any gaps, so we go through."

"Through?" To say Charlie didn't seem keen would have been the understatement of the year.

"Here's how it is." Mac pointed into the minefield. "See how long and narrow that hump is? That tells me they're anti-tank mines designed to blow off tracks. They only operate in excess of four-hundred pounds, you don't weigh more than four-hundred pounds do you?" Mac teased, then continued. "Anti-tank mines are never laid on their own, there will be a scattering of anti-personnel mines with them. The Iraqis lay mines at a ratio of five to one, so there are five anti-tank mines to one anti-personnel, ok?"

Charlie wasn't convinced, "I'm not sure I…"

"Listen fuck-face, you question my judgement again and I'll finish you now; lay up for a day or so, go back and say you got hit, savvy?" Mac's voice softened. "Just do what I say, put your feet where I put mine and everything will be ok, ok?"

Charlie nodded, the pep talk had the desired effect. Either walk through a minefield or face the wrath of the man with the ice cold eyes – no contest. "Ok."

"The minefield will be about a hundred and twenty metres wide. Half an hour at most, let's go." Mac pulled out a two-foot long metal dipstick he'd 'acquired' from a Saudi diesel truck. Holding the dipstick out just above the ground in front of his direction of travel. If there were trip wires he'd hear a metallic 'click' as contact was made giving an indication they were in more trouble than first imagined.

If Pete had had one of these maybe he wouldn't have scalded his dick.

Mac set off, Charlie in tow ten feet behind.

They were over half way across when a flare burst into the sky, Mac dismissed the dull thud as it lit up the sky. He didn't want to look up and ruin his night vision; for some reason everyone seemed to do just that.

Maybe it's just natural human curiosity, anyway, it's too far away to be a problem for us.

Charlie's concentration slipped; he looked skyward, his night vision temporarily impaired. Charlie's foot landed three inches to the left of where Mac had placed his. And his boot nudged a pressure pad, a 'Bouncing Betty' mine flew six feet up into the air and exploded, spraying its deadly contents of shrapnel and ball bearings in a lethal 360° arc.

BOOOM!!

Charlie, being so close to the initial burst was killed instantly. Mac, ten feet away was only spared as his bergan and equipment took the blast and metal hail, the concussive wave knocked him forward and into unconsciousness.

"Ooooh fuckin' shit... what the fu... Ooooh shit."

Mac regained consciousness slowly. His body was wracked with pain and his head felt like Pearl Harbour on a bad day.

He lay on his back and opened his eyes to bright sunlight. Trying to cover his eyes with his hands he found they wouldn't move. Slowly turning his head to the left he saw that his hand was tied to a log, the same log continued behind his neck and his right hand was tied to it also.

Shit, like fucking Jesus on the cross.

Mac tried to sit up but the pain in his head wouldn't allow him to think clearly enough. On the third attempt he managed to get into a sitting position. The pain was so intense he couldn't think why he'd bothered. His face was burned from lying in the sun. He checked his wrist for his watch then his waist for his belt and emergency kit sewn inside it.

Something's not right.

After ten minutes Mac realised what it was. He was naked.

I could really do with a drink.

As if by telepathy the metal door on the far wall swung noisily open. Three large Iraqi soldiers entered; the front one sneered showing rotten teeth. All were dressed in bleached military green.

"Ah," said Mac through the dryness of his throat. "If it isn't Fred and Ginger with room service."

The third of the trio hung back staying near the door. It didn't take them long to get down to business. One sat on Mac's chest while the other produced a pair of rusty pliers. Forcing Mac's mouth open they gripped his top teeth and began to pull. Some teeth were forced out, others broke, pushing the roots out through Mac's gums.

He screamed.

The same pattern was repeated many times. Mac could only guess at how long he was there; the bouts of unconsciousness became a welcome relief. Each time he was visited, the same two would work on him and the third stood by the open cell door. He was the only one armed with a gun – Mac subconsciously noted it was a 9 x 18 Russian Makarov.

At no point did anyone ask him any questions, they just beat him on the soles of his feet and stood on his knees with all their weight pushing the bones and cartilage in a direction they were never meant to go. The pain was immeasurable; sometimes Mac would pass out with the intensity.

Mac awoke from the latest beating; one eye was closed, blood ran from his swollen mouth. He then took stock of his dire situation.

I'm in a cell about fifteen feet square. The walls are about the same height and there's no roof. To stop anyone from climbing over, there are metal spikes pointing downward from the top at an angle of forty-five degrees. Once, sometimes twice a day, two guys come in and soften me up while the third stands by the door ready to shoot me if I try to escape. They've taken me off the log, I guess they figure I'm too weak to make it to the top of the wall. I expect they are softening me up ready for some serious interrogation. Gotta try for the wall.

Mac pulled himself up, his knees were especially painful and swollen twice their usual size. He walked the circumference of the cell trying to block out the pain. He tried to jog but the vibration of his footfalls were just too much to bear and he settled for a brisk walk. Once at the far side of the cell he ran its length before the pain overcame him and launched himself upwards. He didn't make it to the top but did manage to grasp two of the spikes.

Yeah you fuckers.

As he began to pull himself up, unsure of how he'd get past them, one of the spikes, already rusted, began to sag.

Fuck!

Mac plummeted earthward still holding the spike like a runner's baton.

He hit the floor arse first; the jolt knocked him into unconsciousness. Mac didn't know for how long he slept but when he woke it was dusk.

Bollocks. I'm just not able enough to reach the top and even if I did I'm too weak to pull myself over.

He lay there trying to pull his thoughts together through the throbbing ache in his temples, then finally admitted out loud.

"I don't have a plan B."

But, I'm not prepared to have these guys beating down on me. It may seem a little drastic but if I'm gonna go, it's gonna be on my terms. Like Tzun Tsu said, "always give your enemy an avenue of escape. If he cannot escape and must fight, what has he to lose?" That's me, what have I to lose? Only my life but it's on my terms. I'll kill Fred and Ginger but I know the guy at the door will kill me... So fuckin' be it.

Having made the decision to give up his life, Mac felt strangely at peace. The pain in his head and knees subsided, if only a little.

Mac lay facing the far wall in the foetal position; in one hand dust from the floor, in the other, held against his chest, was the spike.

Mac was startled from his light slumber by the grating hinges as the cell door opened.

Wait... wait, speed, timing, technique.

Fred got to Mac's back first, delivering a kick to his kidneys. Mac was so focused he hardly felt it. Waiting for just a fraction longer so Ginger would be close behind Fred, Mac rolled over and stabbed Fred in the balls; deep red blood flowed over Mac's hand and forearm. Using the leverage of the spike still impaling Fred, Mac pulled himself up and threw the dust over Fred's shoulder into Ginger's eyes, pulled out the spike and shoved it into Fred's throat. A wild guttural roar exploded from somewhere, Mac never realised it was from him. Pushing the lifeless Fred to the left, Mac kicked Ginger in the balls; as he doubled over Mac rammed the spike upwards under his chin and into his brain. Mac had practised judo and aikido and taught close-quarter fighting for several years – this was none of those. It was a wild savage slaughter; Fred and Ginger paid dearly for all the beatings Mac had endured.

Slowly coming to his senses Mac realised he was kneeling, covered in blood and fragments of bone and tissue, the mangled remains of the guards all around him. He was crying. His back was towards the cell door, Mac stood and turned, ready to face his certain death as the man with the Makarov would certainly now shoot him.

It took Mac a while to register that the cell door was open but there was no third guard. Mac sniffed then rubbed his nose and eyes.

What the fuck?
Snap to, get a grip, there's no-one there.
Really? Yeah, no-one there.
Think, think you twat… clothes!

Mac went to the bodies and stripped them both; with one jacket he cleaned as much blood off him as possible, the second jacket wasn't as stained as the first. He put it on, then trousers and a pair of over-large boots. Outside the cell door in the corridor was a jug of water and two cups in a recess, just in case the guards got thirsty during beatings. They'd used it to taunt Mac, throwing water in his face and almost letting him have a drink. Mac drank the contents greedily, at the same time scanning the corridor for any other activity. His head swam a little and he steadied himself against the wall. In seconds the feeling passed and he rallied. Still carrying the spike he tiptoed down the dimly lit corridor, past a closed office door, light shining underneath beckoning seductively. Mac tore himself away from the strip of light, then outside into what looked like a small settlement.

It was dark and there were no streetlights, Mac had no idea where he was, he felt certain he was still in Iraq and it wasn't some kind of elaborate mind game but that could just be wishful thinking. He looked into the sky.

Big Dipper… North Star… Keep my back to that and I'm heading south. Eventually I should hit the Saudi border.

With that, Mac started jogging out of the semi-deserted village on the longest journey of his life.

The handcuffs jangled as Mac woke up.
"Where the fuck am…"

"Whoa there son, you're safe, ok, safe. You're in a hospital in Saudi Arabia."

Mac took in the colonel's American Ranger uniform.

"Why am I handcuffed?" he blurted.

"Look at your right hand son, what do you see?"

Mac looked – his right hand still grasped the spike.

"We couldn't get you to let go, so we had to stop you from hurting yourself or anyone else."

Mac slowly opened his hand and the colonel hesitantly took the spike and unlocked the cuffs with keys from his pocket.

"I'll want that back," said Mac an edge to his voice.

"Sure, son. You've had a rough ride, do you remember much?"

Mac told him everything he could remember, from setting off from base to running over several nights to get back to Saudi. The colonel listened intently; Mac had been seconded to the Americans for twelve months, and Colonel Rodriguez was his immediate boss. when Mac had finished the colonel wandered the room, arms folded across his chest.

"Son. I'm not sure you're gonna like what I have to say. That was two months ago."

"What?"

"Do you remember getting back to the border?"

Mac thought for a moment. "No."

"You were delirious. You'd been running for about eight days straight. Your body was completely dehydrated and you lapsed into a coma. The doctors said it was only your will to live that stopped you from dying. You've been in a coma for six weeks. During that time we've extracted the remains of the teeth that were pulled out, contained the spread of infection in your cuts and operated on your knees to reduce the swelling. How good they'll be in the future, well, only time will tell."

"What happens now?"

"Once you're feeling stronger we'll get your teeth capped and have a fuller de-briefing."

"I take it the guy with me didn't make it."

"No, died instantly I'm told." The Colonel patted the bed. "What you did was truly outstanding – well done." Colonel Rodriguez left the room and a few seconds later a female nurse in an intensely white uniform entered.

"You all right?" she asked in a broad Liverpool accent.

"Yeah. Can you do a couple of things for me?"

"I'll try," she said cheekily.

"Can I have a cup of tea?"

"What's the other thing?" she teased, coyly moving closer to the bed. She was used to doing favours for bed-ridden soldiers.

Mac winked. "Pass me that spike."

chapter sixteen

It was at the end of the fifth week since the arson attack on his house when John McBride no longer existed, replaced as he was by his alter ego 'The Wraith.'

It was three in the morning and the normally well lit business area known as Redbank was dark and deserted. The Wraith had spent a week on night recess, checking the gypsy caravan park for the location of the gangs base. He found it on the first night among the discarded fairground rides and dilapidated caravan homes. He had spent the next six nights scouting the area for patterns of behaviour, escape routes and shooting out a couple of street lights each night with a single shot 'Stealth' air gun. He liked the fact that it could be stripped down to small components and when fired made less noise than a gnats fart. Finally he'd created an environment that suited him and he made his move.

Wraith had already spotted the lad who appeared to be the leader of the gang that had fronted him up outside his home. He was also responsible for the arson attack in which little Rachael had almost died. Even now the thought of losing her ran a chill down his spine or maybe it was just the cold night air. Wraith's log of observation had shown a repeated pattern of the leader and, true to form, he was walking the perimeter of the camps fence with Luna his Staffordshire bull terrier cross boxer dog. He wasn't looking for anyone, he liked to walk his dog at night then light up a spliff of bubbleberry near the farthest eastern caravan. That was where the Wraith would make his move and it was during one of his observation stags that he had overheard the leader's street name, 'KR.'

Leaning against the park-home style caravan, KR took a long drag of the spliff and closed his eyes; savouring the sensations it would bring. For a second or two he thought that the tube between his eyes and the shadowy figure behind it were part of his 'trip'. His eyes slowly focused passed the tube and when he saw the skull mask he almost burst into laughter but was brought firmly back top earth when he heard what the voice had to say.

"I know who you are KR and tonight I'm going to kill you," the words were dark and brooding, like a voice from the grave.

"You aint gonna do shi.." KR blustered uncertainly as the long silencer pushed hard into his eye.

"Ok man ok yeah?" the spliff dropped to the floor like a forgotten promise. Wraith's mask had the desired psychological effect, it was unnerving and struck the victim with sufficient instinctive fear as to be a weapon in its own right.

"Good. We understand each other. And just to make sure," Wraith put a gloved hand over KR's mouth to stifle any scream then shot him in the leg.

PHWUT.

"HMMMMMMMPH!"

"I'm gonna take my hand from your mouth. When I do, you stand up straight and keep any smart remarks to yourself. Nod if you understand." KR nodded and although the pain in his leg was more than he could have ever imagined, he did not cry out.

"Good boy," said Wraith and patted him on the cheek patronisingly.

"Now, I'm gonna ask you just one question. If I get the answer I want then you live. If you say anything other than the answer I want then you live with the consequences, right?"

"Wha...?"

PHWUT

The Wraith's second .380 ACP round hit KR in the same leg; a little further down this time.

Pulling his hand away from KR's mouth; he whispered into his ear.

"Last chance bully boy. Nod your head if you understand." he nodded again.

"Are you sure?" he nodded even more vigorously even though the pain brought tears to his eyes, he sniffed and rubbed his eyes with his sleeve.

"Good. Now, my question is... What are the names of the men who were with you five weeks ago when you torched a house by throwing a bottle of petrol through the window. If it helps you remember you threw bricks through the downstairs window on the same day." KR's first thought was to tell the skull that he wasn't a grass and he wasn't going to tell him anything but then he recalled the pain in his leg and the cold eyes behind the mask and decided in a nano-second that he was going to co-operate, and co-operate he did. Not only did he give Wraith the street names of his crew but their real names and some addresses. While all this was going on Luna sat watching, her head tilted to one side with curiosity, she never barked once.

"Good boy," said the Wraith and switched off the tape recorder in his top pocket.

"Now, before we finish; I'm gonna show you something," as he spoke Wraith pushed up the skull mask, even in the dim light KR recognised his face.

"You dat old guy yeah?" just as he recognised John it dawned on him why the skull had wanted the names and also that now he'd seen his face he could no longer be allowed to live.

"Your gonna kill me now init."

PHWUT, PHWUT

Wraith looked down at the crumpled figure.

"You wanna play in the big leagues son; you've gotta up your game."

•••

Becky sat up in the middle of her king-size bed, pillows and soft toys surrounding her. Her favourite soft animal was a teddy bear called Scooby and had pride of place next to her thigh. Since her return a week ago, Nanny had been as attentive as a bull in a field of cows. She seemed not to pause for breath when asking what had happened. Becky insisted she'd fallen from a motorbike, gaining a few cuts and bruises. Nanny was having none of it but didn't pursue the matter, it was not the Sicilian way. Becky knew she'd be fine, the furrows where the 5.56 rounds creased her were healing nicely with no lasting injury. Most of that was due to the doctor Mac had arranged on the flight back.

That's Mac, I hear him now...

"Always plan your escape first," she mimicked his voice, pointing at an imaginary audience. "Remember the three P's, preparation, preparation and preparation."

Becky had seen the look of concern on Mac's face during the flight. It didn't seem to ease even when the doctor said she'd be ok.

If it wasn't for the Kevlar armour Mac had insisted we carry in our bergans, I wouldn't be here now. Where he gets these ideas from I'll never know.

"Hey, Bambino." Nanny's dulcet tones wafted through the hallway like a rasp on a violin. "Zumbodi ta seaa youaa. Make it znappy Big Boy, she gotta eet ya no. Hey, give these to Becky." Nanny handed George a clutch of envelopes and disappeared down the lobby like a mole down a tunnel.

George tapped on the door then entered the bedroom.

"Hi," he said tentatively. He'd called round once before and noticed how much better she was looking this time.

"Hi yourself, 'Big Boy,'" she chuckled.

"Yeah, got a wonderful sense of humour your Nan has. She asked me to give you these." He handed her the envelopes, noticing how much more colour she had in her cheeks.

"Show me both your hands," asked Becky enigmatically.

George obeyed, not understanding.

"See, she must like you... you've still got them." Becky's eyes twinkled in amusement. "So, to what do I owe the pleasure of your company? Didn't think I was seeing you till the weekend?" she asked, looking through the envelopes, recognising Mac's handwriting.

He's never written before?

George looked solemn, Becky caught his mood and didn't like it, she felt apprehensive and placed the unopened envelopes on the bedside table.

"Go on," she goaded.

"Well," he began "It's like this. I've never felt for anyone the way I feel for you…"

Uh oh.

"The work you do with Mac, well, it's obviously dangerous." He held up his hands. "Don't bother denying it, I can see for myself. I just hope to God those aren't bullet wounds."

Becky stared hard at him, waiting patiently for him to finish. George began to nervously pace the bedroom.

"I've thought a lot about what I'm going to say…"

Uh oh.

"…I don't want you to carry on with this life. While you're still young… what I'm trying to say is… I think you and me make a good team. I like spending time with you and I think you like spending time with me. We have great times together and… well… will you marry me?" he finally blurted.

Becky didn't respond; she knew there was more to be said.

"There's one more thing," he said slowly, regaining courage at not being told to fuck off. "If you say yes, then there's no more Mac. No more going away on secretive jaunts. In fact, I'm going to say here and now… it's him or me." with that, George put his hands on his hips in the manner of a general talking to his troops.

Becky sat still in the bed, looking at the folded hands in her lap; the room was deafening in its quiet. Slowly her head rose until she looked directly into his eyes. He noticed her usual black pupils were somehow darker. George involuntarily gulped, his throat felt dry and his palms sweaty as he saw the glistening moisture in her eyes. There was a sureness about her, a definite sense that she knew exactly what she wanted. He smiled a winning smile.

Finally she spoke.

"I'll miss you."

George didn't say a word, just turned on his heel and left. Becky was genuinely sorry he'd made her choose. It really wasn't a choice after all. George was a guy she liked, Mac was a man she loved, more than loved.

"Well," she said to Scooby, her mood rapidly changing. Becky's mind selected and discarded anything that wasn't in the here and now. In an hour or so she'd be hard pressed to remember George's name.

"Let's see what Mac has to say shall we? Just sit there and I'll read you his letter." Becky said jauntily, happy and curious at receiving a letter from Mac.

Reaching over she grasped a tissue and dried her eyes then opened Mac's letter, read the contents, held Scooby close and pulled the covers over her head.

An hour later Nanny walked passed the bedroom door, Becky was still sobbing her heart out.

Nanny shook her head but let her be.

chapter seventeen

Mac sat on his bergan in a shallow dip sipping sugary lukewarm tea from a tin mug.

I haven't had the Iraq dream for years now. I expect it's with what happened to Becky and seeing those guys naked in the cages. On that day when I decided to give up my life, I survived. If Becky had been killed, would I still survive? Probably. Would I want to survive? Probably not.

Right, forget this shit, let's get on with the job.

Mac had gridded the area on his map into fifty metre squares and had spent the last three days searching three-hundred metres. Mac used metres, millimetres, feet and inches indiscriminately, a consequence of being taught feet and inches at school and the metric system in the military; he used whatever came to his mind first. He once caught himself saying a range to a target as, "two miles, one hundred and twenty metres, four feet."

There was no other method that was as thorough as getting down on your hands and knees and crawling in concentric circles until the whole fifty metres was covered. In one day Mac could clear two of the grid squares and had four squares remaining. He would have been able to do more but his knees weren't what they used to be. Mac really had no idea what to expect, a training camp, a base of operations, a hideaway.

No point in theorising the arse out of it. Keep my mind open, that's the best way.

The forest was quite overgrown but Mac used the machete he'd purchased sparingly. He needed to keep noise to a minimum, he could be six feet from someone and he wouldn't know it until the first bullet hit him; stealth was his best friend.

The mountains and forest-cum-jungle he was in was one of the strangest he'd ever encountered. Normally the jungle canopy was so dense overhead that the sun rarely shone on the ground, which kept the floor clear of plants and creepers. Also, you came out paler than when you went in for lack of sunlight. This was very different, the palm fronds and tree boughs didn't intertwine and the trees were spaced quite far apart. The sun penetrated freely and so vegetation grew thickly. Add to this the mountainous terrain, heat, humidity and a never ending supply of insects and you had a very hostile working environment.

All of these thoughts surfaced one by one in Mac's head, but he felt there was something here, something he couldn't put his finger on. He didn't know what it was or where but there was definitely something.

Packing away the mug, Mac rechecked the map, set his Silva compass and headed out in the direction of the next square. After twenty paces Mac stopped, he couldn't hear anything but here there was something... different.

I can't make it out? Is the air denser? Are there less animal noises? What?

Mac slowly crouched down and placed his palm to the warm jungle floor.

Something...? A vibration?

He lay prone, placing his ear to the ground.

Yeah. I can feel it more than hear it, definitely a vibration but from what?

The vibrations were stronger fifteen metres north-west. Mac felt he was on to something and before continuing the search made his way back to his camp where he'd left the bergan and supplies.

Never get separated from your kit: belt order and weapon no more than arm's-length. It's a good maxim.

Resuming his search pattern Mac would go no further than five metres without collecting the bergan. He crawled and intermittently placed his ear to the ground, the vibrations were definitely getting stronger.

Almost an hour went by then, as Mac made his way at ground level through a large ant-laden bush, he saw a grey oval rock.

Where did this come from? It's not volcanic or igneous. It's a different colour from the nearby shale and rockpiles, hmmm.

The rock was about four feet in diameter and around three feet high.

The vibrations are, without doubt, emanating from around this central spot.

Mac stood up and walked around the rock inspecting every clint, gryke and crevice. Satisfied there were no trip-wires or pressure devices he walked forward and tapped the rock.

Bong, Bong.

"Fuck me, it's hollow."

Mac put his arms around the rock and lifted it clear of its housing.

•••

Becky couldn't take staying in bed any longer. She quickly dressed and headed North-East towards Oxford Street in the vain hope that a bit of window shopping would distract her, if only for a moment .

Leaving the apartment she pulled up the hood on her gym top as protection from the rain and strode purposefully out into the night air. The streets were well lit. Becky unconsciously sought the mews streets and back alleys. Head down, hands deep in her front pockets she set a cracking pace. It wasn't long before sweat ran down her spine and was soaked up by the jogging shirt she wore under her top

"I have visual." Don whispered into the Motorola handset from the shadow of a nearby doorway.

"Roger."

"Following on foxtrot, stay parallel and close over."

"Roger out." Guru put his Motorola onto the passenger seat and followed discreetly in the Volvo. He'd memorised a map of the area and would stay parallel, ready to take over from Don if the need arose. Don would give a running commentary as he entered each new sector or street and Guru would plot an intercepting course.

She's taking an erratic course? Seems like she's actively seeking out the darker streets. Maybe she's surveillance-aware, maybe she saw me?... Naw. She's just a girl at college, nothing special about her. She's fit enough, though. The perv was right, wouldn't mind seeing her bent over a wall myself.

"Go foxtrot, keep close, RV rear of Grosvenor, point Victor over."

Two clicks were heard by Don, acknowledgement that the message was received and understood.

Guru quickly parked the car and briskly headed to point Victor.

He must feel he's vulnerable, fuckin' pussy. She's just a bit of skirt, nice arse though. One thing about the perv, he takes a decent photo.

Guru made it to the rear gates of the Grosvenor Hotel, saw the target pass on the far side of the road, Don not too far behind her. Guru tucked himself behind Don, staying on the opposite side of the street, about twenty metres away.

Shit, she's veering off again. This rain helps, everyone keeps their head down and look around far less than usual.

Don saw the target turn down a narrow alleyway between two buildings and closed the gap, fearful he would lose her. As he reached the alleyway's mouth he cursed, she'd gone. It was times like this that he missed having a team to do his bidding. To follow someone effectively he would have had at least four personnel on foot, one on a motorbike and another in a nearby car, every eventuality covered.

Bollocks!

Jogging to the end of the alley in the hope of catching a glimpse of her at the exit, he stopped dead in his tracks, startled by the sudden movement in front.

"Hi. What ya doin'?" Becky asked in a little girl's voice, swaying her shoulders slightly from side to side the way that little girls do when asking grown-ups questions.

"Me? I'm just out for a walk. I..."

Guru entered the alleyway and was silhouetted some ten metres away.

"He just out for a walk too?"

Don was confident, undeterred by this turn of events, after all, she was only a girl.

Guru stayed at the alley entrance, realising he'd been wrong-footed.

Hey, so what! We can stop this pussyfooting around and get some answers from her.

Guru smiled like a wolf, he was looking forward to getting those answers and, if he had to be a bit rough, so much the better.

Becky had spotted Don within a few minutes of leaving her apartment. At first she though he was a flasher or a mugger but he'd kept with her as she increased the pace. She knew better once she'd seen the second man with the limp waiting at the Grosvenors gates.

Gotta find out who they are and what they want. Confrontation seems the quickest technique.

Becky's mind was clear as crystal as she stepped out in front of Don.

"You were on a bridge near Broadland Row some seven months ago. You set off charges by mobile phone. It was a co-ordinated distraction."

"Me? Was I?" In Becky's world that incident was a long forgotten memory; it was nothing, she truly didn't remember.

"Don't get smart with me..." Don then made a very stupid mistake, he stepped forward and raised his hands as if to grab her.

Timing.

Becky moved with startling co-ordination, stepping into his path, grabbed his right wrist, spun into him and dropped vertically exactly the way they'd practised on the beach in Durban. Don flew over Becky's head and shoulders, landing heavily on his sacrum, the lower part of his spine. The pain jolted through his body, Don was momentarily paralysed as his lower vertebrae were crushed. Becky continued the technique, put her arm underneath his chin, lifted, tightened and twisted, his trachea blocked, and with the intense pain in his spine, his body closed down. Don fell quickly unconscious...

Guru couldn't quite make out what was going on. It was reasonable to assume that his boss was getting to grips with her, getting the information they so desperately needed.

He would have to stay where he was and stop anyone from coming down the alley and ruining the interrogation.

Lucky bastard. He always gets the good jobs.

Becky stood up from her kneeling position, her back to Guru. Incredulous, Guru's eyes widened in comprehension as he saw Becky stand, Don, unmoving on the cobbles.

"Fuck." Guru clawed at the shotgun under his overcoat, suspended under his right armpit by a piece of string. The once twenty-six inch barrels now a more manageable twelve.

In the confines of the alleyway and at this distance she won't stand a chance.

Becky spun on her axis, right hand moving to the Spectre in her waistband. She turned, threw, already knowing that he was at the limit of her expertise. The shotgun began to gain height and bear on her as the Spectre thudded its full blade length just below his sternum.

Nothing fancy, go for the centre of the body mass.

Speed.

Becky was right behind the blade, launching herself like a cheetah after its morning prey. Guru almost forgot about the shotgun as his hands tried to pull out the blade embedded in his chest.

'Ow did this 'appen? Fuck... 'n' she's only a bit o' skirt.

His head tilted downward; centred on the excruciating pain, he would never be able to appreciate her perfectly executed Togakure ryu ninjutsu style.

Technique.

The technique Becky called upon was from the skills of daken-taijutsu , a powerful front kick delivered from a high leap. Becky's foot caught Guru just below his throat on his clavicle bone, winding and stunning him at the same time. Simultaneously while executing the technique Becky pulled the knife free, landed low on the ground and stabbed Guru in the femoral artery on the inside of his upper leg. Blood gushed over her hand as her would-be assailant lost two pints of blood in half as many seconds. Guru fell to the floor in immediate shock from the huge loss of blood, his death but a lingering moment away.

Becky stood over the prone figure taking care not to get any of rapidly growing blood pool on her new trainers, Guru's eyelids fluttered in the throes of death. Searching his pockets for any means of identification, Becky was curious as to who these two were.

It worked again. Speed, timing and technique, shame I can never get them in the right order. Nothing on him. Well, nothing except this cheap Motorola radio. You can buy these from any Carphone Warehouse or mobile phone store. These aren't from any of the three-digit services. MI5, CIA, NSA, MI6. Definitely operating on a shoe string. I'll bet they were private investigators or contractors, something like that.

Becky pulled the shotgun free, examined it then tossed it into a nearby puddle, destroying any fingerprints or DNA.

Oh well, nothing like a good workout to clear the mind, that's what Mac used to say... oh crap. So much for putting him out of my mind. Right, focus, focus. What was I doing? Oh yes, window shopping.

With that thought Becky washed the Spectre in the same puddle she'd thrown the shotgun into, put it back in her waistband and sauntered, without so much as a backward glance, off to look at dresses in the House of Fraser window displays.

Don had made a move towards Becky and was unconscious. Guru had upped the ante and gone for a weapon – that changed everything and was the reason he was now dead. Becky had no compunction about killing him, after all, she reasoned, it was his decision, not hers.

●●●

Mac found himself in a store room, shelves lined with foodstuffs, water and spare parts for what looked like microprocessor boards. Taking a closer look it quickly became apparent that all of the canned goods were of American origin.

Curiouser and curiouser.

Before continuing further Mac replaced the ventilation grill on the air-conditioning duct that he'd crawled through just in case anyone came into the room and saw it off its housing. They could raise the alarm and Mac's unseen advantage would be lost.

That twenty-metre rope I brought really came in handy in getting down the shaft that was covered by fake rock. I wonder what all this is about? Osama's underground bunker? HQ? Training school? I don't even know where to begin.

Mac listened at the door. All he could hear was the steady hum of electrical machinery and ventilation fans.

Twisting the door handle Mac was pleasantly surprised to find the door unlocked.

Slowly pulling the door ajar an inch, Mac's eyes scanned the long cavernous interior ablaze with artificial light from the long overhead fluorescent tubes and what looked like six-foot-high steel grey lockers. Mac's brow knitted.

Wardrobes? Lockers?!!

The floor was covered in ceramic tiles alternating light grey and an off-white. Large mirrored windows sectioned off the cavern from sleeping and cooking quarters, the door ajar. There was an unmade bed inside and a couple of Playboy magazines on view.

At the far end of the underground warehouse Mac could make out the solitary figure of a male standing on a pair of step-ladders changing a bulb in a wall-light. Mac watched as the man, dressed in a grey boiler suit, came down from the ladders and walked in-between the lockers, flitting a brush across the towers and closely checking the surfaces for dust and grit.

He seems to be the only occupant. No cameras on any of the walls and I can't see any other external doors. What's this all about? I need info and he's the one who'll provide it.

Mac silently closed the door behind him, Remington shotgun at the ready. Criss-crossing in-between the tall grey oblongs Mac now saw they weren't lockers at all but computer towers, some with magnetic tape spools, whirring, feeding information to a mainframe hidden somewhere else in the complex. Red, blue and green lights flashed randomly accompanied by the odd beep.

Making less noise than a shadow, it didn't take Mac long to get behind the unsuspecting caretaker, engrossed as he was in his spring cleaning. Stepping out from cover Mac hit the grey-garbed man in the small of the back with the extended butt of the Remington. He fell forward, first to his knees then to his face as a second blow was delivered between his shoulder blades.

The caretaker turned slowly, painfully, to face his attacker then pushed himself along the polished floor with his hands and feet in a crab-like manoeuvre. Finally reaching the wall some ten feet away, he could go no further, his face a picture of surprise and fear.

"Who... what...? who the...?"

Mac knelt so that their eyes made contact.

"Hi. I'm impressed," he said conversationally.

"The place is spotless. You must spend what? Ten hours a day cleaning?"

Caretaker mouthed words but made no sound. Mac held up his hand to quell any questions.

"Let me guess. I'm usually a good guesser." Mac said without warmth.

"You're just a guy who cleans up the place. You know nothing about what really goes on here. And, there's no way that you can tell me anything about these computers. That about right?"

Caretaker's eyes flicked left and right, away from Mac's piercing gaze. Mac tapped him on the foot, keeping him focused.

"I said, that about right?"

"Yeah," answered the prone figure, "that's right."

"So. Let's be crystal clear about this. You stay here all alone. You clean the computers, make your own food and you never see anyone else. You wouldn't know one end of a computer from another. You're a nobody who knows nothing. Right?"

"Yeah," he said gaining confidence, "a nobody, that's right."

"Hmm." Mac's eyes sank into his head as he considered the surprised man's replies.

Like a striking cobra, Mac's hand sprung forward; in it, as if by magic, was the D-Day blade which sank into the man's shoulder quicker than a bolt of lightening.

"Arghh... You fuckin'..."

"Now, now. There's no need for profanity." Mac hissed, swatting the man's hand away with his left arm.

He sounds American. Arizona or some other cowboy state. Interesting. What the hell could be the link between Osama Bin Laden and the United States besides the obvious?

"I need you to listen to me. I do have your complete attention, don't I?"

"You fuckin'... Arghhh." Mac twisted the cruciform blade slightly.

"I said..."

"Yeah, yeah." Spittle ran down his chin and his eyes glazed over.

"In the storeroom there are micro-processor boards, giga-sized hard-drives and mono-filament wires. So, my question is, if you're here alone, who replaces these computer components when they break? You do see my point, don't you?"

"Wha..ARGHHHHH." Mac twisted the knife. The cruciform blades grated individually against his collar bone. The intense agony was like nothing he had ever known. He felt the vibration and grating sensation even in his mouth. It was like having a round file rotating over clenched teeth, bits of enamel being ripped off by the hard metal. Mac straddled the immobile figure to keep him from thrashing around.

"Ok, ok, fuckin' ok! Yeah, yeah, it's me, ok. Stop, stop, please stop," he gasped with pain. Mac wasn't sure how much more the man's heart could take.

He certainly isn't a spook or Special Forces. There's not enough muscle on him. I'd guess he hardly works out at all.

Tears of fear and pain ran down his cheeks. Mac had broken him quickly, not knowing how long he had. Mac stood, leaving the man where he was.

"So. What's all this about?" Mac waved at the room.

"I've... I've been here for four months." He took deep breaths and pressed his hand against the seeping wound.

"We all do a six month tour."

"We?"

"Yeah. One guy at a time. There's only ever one of us. We've gotta keep the place clean, computers don't like dust and if there's a breakdown, we're trained to repair it."

"Ok, you're a caretaker. A caretaker of what?"

The man in grey hesitated fractionally. Mac took a step forward and hefted the knife.

"Ok, ok," he said, holding his uninjured arm as though it would throw up a force-field that would stop Mac.

"These computers are tapped into Echelon and Mercury..."

Two of the world's most sophisticated electronic surveillance systems.

"...every telephone conversation, every email in the world is re-routed through these computers. It's analysed and anything that includes 'trigger' words or phrases is re-analysed."

"What happens then?"

"It's passed to the Central Chamber," he replied, as though it was explanation enough.

"What does the Central Chamber do?" Mac asked gently, patiently.

"It makes decisions and sends out instructions."

"Who to?"

Grey man found a small piece of resolve and stubbornly clung to it. Mac lifted him up from the floor and pushed him forward.

"Take me to the Central Chamber," he ordered.

It makes you wonder if any of the 'Big Boys' are tapped into the feed for this place? Choicepoint and Accuint are two data-gathering companies that immediately spring to mind. The sheer size of those entities is mind-boggling and this type of information would be right up their street.

Grey man walked unsteadily towards an unassuming door. Mac noticed he was limping and recollected what he'd been told years before.

When people sustain an injury that cannot be readily identified, they will limp. This is a psychosomatic reaction, they will not even realise they are doing it. It is in the hope that people at a distance will recognise they are injured and be sympathetic.

Grey man opened the door, Mac close behind. The room was much smaller at around ten metres square. A single bank of twelve magnetic tapes spooled frenetically on one wall, while at the room's centre was a steel desk, single stool and monitor screen with a keyboard underneath. Grey man looked at the monitor then at the man who had caused him so much pain. Mac recognised the look behind his eyes.

He knows. He fuckin' knows.

"Tell me about the monitor," asked Mac, as though an aside.

"You'd be more interested in the bank of..." Mac cut him off sharply.

"You need to realise. You're only alive because I will it. Do you understand?"

Grey man looked to the floor, defeated.

"Say it!" Mac snapped. Grey man jumped.

"I understand," he said almost inaudibly.

"Good. Now, tell me about the monitor."

"The console can be used to check if programs are working at optimum efficiency. As a consequence, program headings can be displayed."

"You can tell me what it's working on?"

"Yes. And also what it has been working on since it was switched on in '95, eleven years ago."

"Show me the latest headings," said Mac, intrigued.

Grey man sat on the stool and pressed various keys on the board. It wasn't long before the current headings were displayed.

Mac leant forward, he needed to read every last word.

"Fuck me!" he exclaimed uncharacteristically then pointed to the screen.

"Show me that heading."

Grey man complied and in seconds page after page of operational details, names, locations, equipment caches and bank accounts showing usable funds appeared. Mac's eyes hungrily absorbed the information.

"That one. Show me that one." Mac touched the screen in his eagerness. Details sprang up.

"Fuckin' unbelievable," Mac said under his breath. The information he'd seen physically took his breath away. It took him a minute to recover from the shock and realisation of what he'd seen.

"Print everything!"

"I can't, there are no printers. And before you ask, I can't delete, download or transfer it anywhere. It's a read-only file." Mac looked at him, his body language screaming he was telling the truth.

"Ok. Show me everything, and I mean everything."

Mac sat on the stool that grey man had vacated. His head swam with the ramifications of what he'd learned. He felt sick and his skin was clammy. Grey man stood uncertainly on the other side of the desk. Neither spoke for a very long sixty seconds.

"Can you re-program these headings?"

"No, sorry."

"But you can add to them, can't you?"

"Yeah. I could add to them. I suppose that would change the parameters." He stroked his chin thoughtfully.

"Ok. Come round here. This is what I want you to do."

chapter eighteen

Natalie didn't normally drink alcohol but tonight was going to be a night for changes, but not necessarily the changes she'd been expecting.

She'd met up with Toby at the main entrance just as they'd agreed. She thought he looked great in a wide-collared light cream shirt, white trousers and a pair of brown leather deck shoes, his well-groomed light brown hair almost touching his shoulders – in every way, the typical university 'jock' but with brains too. Her father hadn't asked too many questions when she'd told him she was going to go for a run and burn off the day's excitement, then have an early night. After a quick but thorough shower she dressed in a pair of tight black Lycra trousers and a dark blue top that only just made it around her comparatively large 32C breasts, a pair of Nike Air trainers rounded off the outfit. Hardly catwalk material but the best she had.

So far the night had been perfect. They'd been for a seafood special at a local restaurant – crystal prawns, lobster and monkfish – then onto a nightclub where they danced and drank until the small hours. Natalie danced with such sensuality and abandon that when she opened her eyes she saw Toby open-mouthed with disbelief; a smile readily took its place as she recognised the look of lust on his face. Natalie had laughed so much during the evening that her jaw ached.

I've never felt so good, so alive. I know it's stupid and I've only just met the guy, but I really like him. I hope he wants to take me home. I really think I could make his night. And I hope he can make mine too.

Toby had excused himself a couple of times by saying he was phoning his mother and checking she was all right; Natalie thought that was sweet.

At three in the morning Toby had suggested they go back to his beach-house; Natalie readily agreed.

It's been a fantastic night and it's about time I lost my virginity.

It was a fifteen minute drive to the beach-house. Once through the door they kissed. Natalie wanted to take off Toby's shirt and get right to it but he asked her to wait and led her upstairs. She was giggling with excitement and expectation as they reached the landing. Toby opened a door to the bedroom and gently pushed her in front of him, closing the door behind them in the darkened room.

"Now what?" she giggled, her voice low with expectation.

"Gotta surprise for ya," he said, his voice seeming a little detached.

"Toby?" there was something in the tone of his voice that she didn't like.

Suddenly the lights were switched on, bathing the room in stark brightness. She blinked rapidly as her eyes adjusted.

Sitting around the room were a further eight men, all smiling lascivious, lecherous smiles, all with undisguised lust in their eyes. Natalie was confused.

"What's going on?" she asked uncertainly. Toby stepped forward.

"Well, I figure it this way. You were gonna have sex with me, in fact you were happy to do it. So, as I'm a kinda share 'n' share alike guy I thought I'd invite a few close friends around, 'n' ya know... share."

"You thought because I'd sleep with you I'd sleep with anybody, that it?" The alcohol dispersed from her bloodstream instantaneously as anger burned in the pit of her stomach. Anger at the men sitting around the room but mostly anger at herself for being duped so easily.

That's what he was doing when he made the phone calls, he was organising this!

"Well, I think—"

"HEY! You're not here to think baby. You're here to suck 'n' fuck..." Toby pointed his finger at her accusingly. As if on cue, two of the onlookers stepped forward and grabbed her arms, trying to pull her to the ground. The others crowded around eager to grab at her young flesh.

For just a second it looked as though these evil men were about to have their way with her. The initial shock had deadened her usual instinctive reflexes. It was as if she was lost, drowning in the morass of their sexual appetite then, for the second time in twelve hours, Natalie once again felt a warm breeze on her face.

•••

Within two weeks of KR's 'interview' the remaining five members of the crew that had participated in the arson attack were dead. In three of five cases the police put it down to inter-gang rivalry, in one it was a murder they would never solve and the last one they put down as a missing person even though they had a feeling he would never be found.

The Wraith had taken care of those who would do harm to his family and he began to think that he might eventually lead a normal life. Four days after the final crewmember had been dealt with John returned from taking Rachael to school to find a brown A4 size envelope had been pushed under his door. Living in a secure building John thought that it must be an internal circular maybe informing all the residents of maintenance work to be carried out. He placed it on the hall stand and would get round to reading it during his 'NAAFI' break after the housework.

Later, after having made himself a toasted bacon sandwich and coffee, he collected the day's mail and sat in the living area. The large brown envelope was opened last and when John looked at the contents he gave an audible gasp. Inside were six large black and white photos each showing one member of the crew he had killed and a sheet of paper that read...

MEET AT 9PM TODAY AT ANGEL MEADOW PARK, COME ALONE.
"Shit!"

It had been dark for an hour by the time the man reached the park. He had dressed for the cold November night in a long dark brown overcoat, Homburg hat and a Cambridge University scarf that he'd picked up at an Oxfam shop for two pounds. As the figure waddled around the perimeter he tried to read the information boards that dotted the path explaining how the park had come into being. It appeared that Angel Meadow Park had originally been a part of the Girls Home above the nearby Charter Street Ragged School that had been opened by the Duchess of Sutherland after the First World War. Before that it had been a cemetery and church, some of the original gravestones were still occupying a portion or the park, many of the graves dated back to 1793 and even earlier. One of the boards stated "The lowest, most filthy, most unhealthy and vile in the locality of Manchester is called Angel Meadow. A place of prostitutes, their bullies, thieves, cadgers and vermin. They are the very worst sites of filth and darkness."

Hmm. If one believed everything they read in the Manchester Evening News the place doesn't appear to have changed much since then.

Checking his watch he found it was twenty seconds after six.
"You wanted to see me?"
The man visibly jumped, he prided himself on having acute hearing and had never heard the speaker approach.
"I see you live up to your name Mr. McBride."
"My name?"
"Wraith. Please; walk with me." John's curiosity couldn't have been more piqued.
"If you're the police I'll come quietly, there's no need to bring in armed response. I..."
"One moment," the man interrupted. "There's no need to involve the local authorities, let me explain. I represent an organisation that could use your skills. I have read your military

history and a full dossier on your latest, shall we say... campaign?"

"But I..."

"Please," the man held up his hand to curtail further denials. "The United Kingdom is riddled with such people. I can understand your motives maybe even the one's that you are not aware of yourself. I want to offer you a job."

"Doing what?" John hadn't yet caught on.

"You have a little girl, Rachael? I know you wouldn't like to leave her for very long and so, I want to offer you work here in the UK. There is a selection and training phase that you must first complete and after that you will work only for me."

"I don't get it? Doing what?"

"Killing my dear boy," he patted John on the arm fatherly. "It's what you do best."

four months later

The Wraith waited patiently in the bushes. He'd been in location since 3am; a little under five-hours and it was a freezing February morning. His camouflage streaked unbreakable flask with its coffee contents had taken a bashing. The hot sweet tea had helped keep him alert during his vigil. Wraith had relieved himself in a plastic half-litre Coca-Cola container and a funnel that he'd brought specifically for the occasion and would take away with him when he'd finished this particular operation.

What goes in must come out.

The street lights had not long been extinguished but it wasn't yet completely light. The man Wraith was waiting for was unusual in that he was the only drug dealer he knew who rose early in the morning to make his Mother breakfast. She lived three streets away from where Danny the drug dealer lived, the Wraith had followed him on two previous nights expecting Danny to lead him to his supplier but Danny was clever and so far the main supplier had eluded him.

Danny was of medium height and build and in is late twenties with the ubiquitous grotty baseball cap, the only thing that distinguished him from the usual crowd was that he invariably wore gloves. The Wraith had discovered that Danny had a skin condition called eczema and to avoid his flaky skin falling into food or contaminating any other produce he wore protection. Danny's house was a modest end-of-terrace in Salford whilst his mother's residence was a detached three bedroomed affair with well maintained gardens and a wooden fence all the way around.

Over the five-days that the Wraith had been watching his target he'd been impressed with Danny's loyalty and devotion towards his ailing Mother. The Wraith knew that Danny was as good as dead, he could have killed him on several occasions but in the final analysis the Wraith decided on a different course of action.

As Danny entered the pin number into the coded front gate the Wraith hopped over the rear fence, ran the length of the garden and climbed in through an unlocked window that he had prepared the night previously.

This place's furnishings look like their stuck in a nineteen-fifties time warp.

There was the usual lamp stand in one corner with a frilly shade. A picture of a pretty Asian girl in a faded white frame and three blue ducks each one getting larger as they flew towards her. On the mock-marble mantelpiece were knick-knacks and ornaments from such far-flung places as Liverpool and Bournemouth.

I wonder if the set designer from Coronation Street knows this place exists. He could get a lot of inspiration from it.

As Danny entered by the front door Wraith was taking the stairs noiselessly two at a time. As Danny opened the fridge door with his gloved hand and took out two eggs for his Mother's breakfast Wraith waited patiently on the landing. Danny fried the eggs and placed them on the toast, put the teapot and breakfast on a tray and began to walk up the stairs. The Wraith opened Danny's Mother's bedroom door and took a soft chair in the room's corner where Danny would not immediately look as he opened the door. Mother was propped up on several pillows with her eyes shut, she never heard or saw Wraith as he took his position.

Within moments Danny entered balancing a breakfast laden

blue floral tray on one hand, Mother's eyes opened on cue as the daily ritual began.

"Morning Mum; sleep well?" He placed the tray on her lap.

"As well as can be expected these days." There was an unmistakable unspoken sigh.

"I've done your favourite today Mum." Danny did the same breakfast every day.

"Thanks Son." Mum shivered. "A bit of a chill in the air today, what's the weather like?"

"Looks like there's a storm coming," whispered Wraith from the corner seat.

Danny almost threw the tray over his Mother with surprise. Mother hardly moved.

"Who's your friend Danny? I don't remember you saying anything about bringing a friend," she asked sleepily already tired from the exertion of answering her son.

Danny had been shocked by the apparition but thought he'd better play it down so as not to upset his Mother.

"Yeah mate, who are you my friend?" Danny wasn't at all as confident as he sounded.

"Don't you remember Danny? You asked me to call round and meet your Mum. Then you said that after I'd done that we'd go downstairs and talk about your past and your future." Wraith smiled like a Tiger watching a Gazelle that had no chance of escape.

"Yeah that's right. Listen Mum you eat your breakfast while I go downstairs and talk to my friend, yeah?" Danny kissed his Mother on the forehead and went to the door, Wraith followed closely behind.

Once in the living room Danny turned but was careful not to do it too quickly; he'd assessed this man could be dangerous, he didn't know the half of it.

Wraith held his hand up.

"Before you say anything I want you to listen to me without interruption, nod if you understand me."

Danny nodded; he didn't like the look of this man at all.

He's got dead eyes, he scares the shit outta me but I can't let him know.

"Danny. I was sent here today to kill you." Danny's face turned white, he believed him. "You sell drugs, drugs that are strangling the population of the UK and I'm here to stop you. While I've been watching you I've come to understand a little of what you do and why you do it and, although it goes against the rules, I'm going to give you a chance to change your ways." Wraith paused but Danny was listening and wasn't that stupid he'd interrupt.

"I want you to work for me Danny. I want you to tell me everything you know about everyone you know. Who sells what and who buys it. Everything. Do you understand me?" Danny nodded.

"Do you have any questions, you can speak now."

Danny was silent for a few moments as he digested what had been said.

"You want me to be a grass," it wasn't a question.

"That's one way of putting it, I have another."

"I'm listenin'."

"You would be my accomplice, my helper if you like. You have the kind of street knowledge that I can never have. You've been brought up into this way of life. You know people, places and what's going on behind closed curtains. You'll be my Ace-in-the-hole."

"It's still a grass."

"No, you'll be an informant and anyway look at the alternative." Wraith's voice could freeze sand dunes; it sent a chill down Danny's spine. "You'll be dead. Your Mother will waste away or be put in a home where she'll quickly follow you. If you come in with me you won't have to sell drugs to keep your mum in this house and you'll have enough money to employ a full-time nurse."

Danny's face lit up.

"No more drugs and my mum can have constant attention? Sounds too good to be true." Danny wanted to be convinced.

"I promise you Danny, if you become my source of information everything I've said will happen. The nurse will be here by tomorrow and your financial worries will be over."

Danny turned to face the wall.

"What happens to the people that I ...inform on?"

"They die Danny."

He turned back to the Wraith.

"If you'd have lied to me I would have fucked you right off."

Wraith sighed, "I know Danny; I know."

•••

"Here's the report you wanted in respect of Doctor Haidar and his whereabouts." Helen handed the director a beige folder.

"Who did you send?"

"Detective-Sergeant George. Solid, dependable, has done good work for us in the past. He was briefed not to hold back on his technique and that we needed the information soonest."

"Hmm." Henry opened the folder and read the three page report in a matter of seconds.

"It says here that Doctor Haidar was summoned late on the evening of sixteenth July 1996 by Dodi Fayed's personal assistant. He was told it was a matter of professional urgency and he was required to attend Princess Diana as she had been taken ill without prior warning. A car arrived and took him directly to Stansted airport where a private jet took him to Monaco."

"Seems to be very well organised doesn't it?" said Helen.

"Yes, but nothing sinister in that. On arriving at Monaco airport the doctor was again met by a car and taken to a large house somewhere near the French border, about an hour's drive from the airport. When he arrived he was taken to the study where he was given refreshments. Here he waited for two hours before Dodi Fayed appeared and thanked the doctor for his prompt arrival and was then informed that the situation had stabilised during his flight and his services were no longer required."

"It does seem an awful long way to go just to be told the patient's got better."

"Yes, it does."

"The doctor continues... that he was given a cheque for one-hundred thousand pounds and told that this matter should never be discussed again. The doctor thought it odd, but he hadn't broken the Hippocratic oath so shrugged his shoulders and took the cheque along with a return flight home. Having missed the meeting at Kings he spoke with the Dean, giving the excuse of having a grumbling appendix and booked two extra dates as recompense."

"But it still doesn't answer our original question does it?"

"You mean, why was he summoned in the first place?"

"Yes."

"No. The real question is – what kind of illness is it that has you at death's door one minute and a short flight later, you've recovered?"

Henry continued to stare at the far wall as his mind worked on the problem parameters. He took off his reading glasses and pinched the bridge of his nose, suddenly overwhelmed at the enormity and complexity of the variables before him. Helen saw the exhaustion written into his every movement.

"You need to go home and have a rest," she said quietly.

"Rest? Rest! When the very fabric of our great nation is in jeopardy." Henry's zeal was the equal of any would-be-terrorists or fanatic.

Helen's quiet demeanour abruptly changed.

"Now you just listen to me you pompous ass." She leaned forward over the desk and pointed her finger like a magic wand. "Who do you think you are? You're always saying how no-one is indispensable, well that goes for you too. Now, take your hat and coat" – she lifted them off the door hook and threw them at him – "go home, get a good night's sleep and come back at eight tomorrow morning with a fresh outlook and a similar complexion."

Henry was aghast but was quick enough to notice the steely glint in her eyes and the set of her jaw.

This must be the look she would give the IRA bombers when they questioned her orders.

He knew she had his best interests at heart and quickly grasped the notion that resistance would be futile. He nodded assent and grudgingly put his arms through the long overcoat.

"Eight a.m. sharp," he said with mock severity, hoping for the last word.

"And not a second sooner." She stood between Henry and the computer monitors ensuring he could not say a last farewell.

He opened his mouth as if to speak then closed it again as he realised he would not win this argument.

Once Henry had gone, Helen switched off the office lights and locked the door with the only key.

If he thinks he can come back here after I'm gone then he's in for a surprise. I'll be here at seven fifty-five and if he's any sooner he'll just have to wait.

●●●

"What's that?" Mac asked loudly, trying to make himself heard over the ear-splitting siren. He knew grey man hadn't pushed a hidden button or anything as he'd had him in his peripheral vision all the time.

"Shit, I forgot. Look man I'm sorry. I should have remembered."

"Remembered what?"

He reached inside his grey overalls and pulled out a small pager-sized black box that had been fixed to his belt.

"It works on the same principle as the ones New York cops have. If they're prone for more than thirty-seconds, it sends out a call for help. When I was on the floor it would've activated. The cavalry's on the way, the siren means that air movement has been detected. They'll be overhead in a chopper. Look man, I'm sorry, they make us wear it in case we have a heart attack or an accident or something," he pleaded, getting more anxious by the second as he saw the darkness cloud Mac's eyes.

"Hey, no problem, we all make mistakes. It's just, some mistakes have greater consequences than others." Mac shot him in the chest. No-one ever survives a 12-gauge round at close range. Grey man was punched backwards, his cleaning days well and truly behind him.

Rather than waste valuable time searching for an exit Mac ran back to the storeroom and pulled off the ventilation grill. His rope was still hanging where he left it and he scurried up the sisal like a monkey after bananas. He knew the clock was ticking.

If the reinforcements can't make contact with the caretaker I expect the place will be blown by remote control. There's no way the American intelligence agencies can let this compound be found, not ever.

As he climbed out of the vent Mac glimpsed skyward.

An Mi-24 Hind – that usually means a total of eight passengers, but in this case it'll have six heavily armed guys on board with lots of equipment. They'll be directed from above. I need to stay directly below so it can't bring to bear the 12.7 machine gun or either of the 80 millimetre rocket pods. The bubble on the underside is a thermal imager and they'll be gettin' my location through their comms system right about now. The chopper's around two-hundred metres up and almost straight above me.

Mac smiled as he ejected the cartridge from the Remington's chamber and thumbed in a Bolas round then closed the action.

Pointing vertically, Mac loosed the shotgun's deadly payload. As it left the muzzle, the cartridge split and two half-ounce steel balls connected by a 12-inch razor-sharp flexible steel wire slowly, inexorably, began to spin. The Hind was from the former Soviet Union and purchased along with several others as deniable transport. They were invulnerable to small-arms fire, the underside of the helicopter being encased in a lightweight military-grade titanium alloy.

It was not the helicopter's body that Mac had aimed for but the bigger target, rotor blades. A single round may not have hit them but the Bolas round was now a spinning arc of 12-inches. They hit the rotor blades close to the housing, slicing into one of the blades: the nick was enough to cause a fracture which, because of the rotational strain on the blades, caused enough vibration to wrench it clean from its gearing. The helicopter tilted violently to the left and began to lose altitude. As the pilot fought for control the sliced blade flew through the air and hit the stabilising rotor on the rear tail. Whatever control the pilot had was now gone. Mac saw an ashen face lean out of the co-pilot's window before the chopper dipped behind a ridge and crashed to the jungle floor in a tremendous roar of exploding fuel and ammunition.

I won't be so lucky as to have the whole team aboard. They will have abseiled down ropes the minute they got here. At least they've lost their eye in the sky and I'd expect them to close in on the last location they were given... me.

Mac looked for cover as he saw movement in his peripheral vision. Keeping low, Mac snaked his way along the ground with an agility that surprised even him. Troops in jungle camouflage could be seen moving towards his last location in an extended line. He peered through the foliage trying to get a bearing on the slow moving patrol.

They're cautious, good. That'll give me some time.

Mac silently ejected the spent Bolas cartridge and inserted a 'Dragon's Breath' round.

They're not going to like this... fuck 'em.

Sighting along the extended line's length, Mac pressed the trigger. The six Special Forces personnel had their M4 assault rifles and Minimi Machine gun in their shoulders at the 'ready' position; any moment now they expected to see the enemy, none of them realised they'd already been flanked.

Shooting out to a distance of over one-hundred feet, the magnesium and phosphorous round simulated the effects of a flame-thrower. The three nearest soldiers caught much of its effect and fell to the ground writhing and screaming as their skin was burned away from their flesh. Small explosions burst outward from each of the burning figures as ammunition and grenades in their assault vests exploded due to the tremendous heat.

That's why they call it Dragon's Breath.

As soon as he'd fired, Mac scrambled away on his stomach. He hated leaving the Remington with its barrel sticking out from the outcrop but the remainder of the patrol had to have something obvious to shoot at and the flames from the muzzle had already given away his position. Thick grey-black smoke from the flaming flora and trees helped with confusion but these guys were good and immediately laid down accurate suppressing fire as they tried desperately to ignore the wails and sobs from their fallen comrades.

Finding a small stream bed Mac 'monkey crawled' quickly to another firing position. He'd hit them with enfilade fire, now he'd try defilade fire with the Tokarevs.

It had been many years since he'd been at the School of Infantry in Warminster, being run ragged by instructors. The lessons of enfilade, fire along an enemy's length and defilade, fire along an enemy's depth, had been covered in detail. To Mac, it seemed like yesterday.

Resting the magazine housings on a clump of grass, Mac sighted the pistols then emptied both magazines into the general area of the remaining patrol members. One was hit in the stomach, another in the thigh. Mac quickly changed positions and magazines as he ran. The 7.62x25 rounds were devastatingly powerful, gaping wounds were made that needed immediate attention. Checking the area he'd fired on from a fern-laden vantage point, Mac could see the remaining patrol member giving medical aid to his fallen comrades as they writhed in agony from wounds to the stomach and shoulders.

That'll keep him busy. He won't leave them and come after me – that's not the way they do things.

Mac crawled backwards into dead ground, checked his compass and headed out of the 'contact' area. He felt more for the loss of the Remington than he did for the devastated Special Forces patrol.

•••

The Director caught a cab outside Whitehall and gave an address in Chelsea. Once at the given location the Director paid the driver and walked several streets before hailing a second cab and giving an address in Bayswater.

As the second cab drew off, the Director waited for it to turn the corner before he waddled down a side street, turned right and stopped at a large terraced house in a quiet pedestrianised area of the Bayswater district. Without pause he unlocked the door and entered the dimly lit hallway. Continuing without breaking pace, Henry unbolted the rear door and wandered into the garden where he took a right through the broken fence and up to the rear door of the property adjacent to the one he'd originally entered. Here Henry paused and lifted a corner of the coconut mat; as he expected, there was a solitary Yale key, bright and shiny. He ignored the key and opened the letterbox, placing his left hand inside until it lay flat on a cold metal surface. After several clicks, the door swung open and Henry entered. The key was a decoy. Should anyone put the key in the lock they would have been greeted with a shock of seventy-five thousand volts and a silent alarm would have alerted a dedicated department.

The door closed automatically behind him and Henry was immediately confronted by a steel mesh wall that was bolted to the walls, ceiling and floor of the rear hall. Set into the mesh was a panel of press-numeric-digits. Henry knew he had only twenty-seconds in which to enter the correct six-digit number, if he failed to do that within the time limit, sleeping gas would be pumped into the area he was standing and a vehicle borne VIP Protection Team would be at the premises in under a minute. The code was his wife's birthday reversed 05-20-62. A number and sequence he was never likely to forget.

Once through the security measures Henry shrugged off his coat, poured himself a small single malt whisky and sat heavily in the large over-stuffed chair.

As he sipped the tingling nectar his eyes slowly moved to the black and white photograph of a female on the shelf of the grey marble fireplace.

Henry's eyes slowly watered as years of memories washed over him, memories he'd long ago pushed to the back of his mind.

My dearest Margaret, how I miss you so.

Henry remembered the night over twenty years ago when he'd received a telephone call to say she'd been killed. He was stunned, so stunned in fact that he lost consciousness and was roused only by the ringing of the doorbell.

I'll never find another woman like her.

Not that he'd ever looked. Margaret's death was like having part of himself amputated without his consent. He was, for many years, inconsolable.

It had been Helen at the door all those years ago... Helen. What would I do without you?

Over a period of days Henry had pieced together what had happened to his wife. During the school holidays Margaret, as a local teacher, would volunteer her services with an international aid organisation and she would spend six weeks, sometimes longer, teaching basic English language skills to Ethiopians, Afghanis or anyone who wanted to learn. She was passionate about teaching and would work 18 to 20 hours a day with her pupils.

One bright sunny day in the foothills of Somalia her morning class was interrupted by an armed gang who wanted to take all boys over the age of eight to their training camp where they could be trained as followers of the Somalian Independence Front, where they would be used as cannon-fodder against the government troops.

Astounded at their effrontery and arrogance Margaret forgot the advice given to working nationals which was one of non-confrontation. She pulled the young boys close and stood between them and the grinning gang who quickly tired of the interfering white woman and shot her dead. The boys, some wailing with fear, meekly fell in line and were marched off into the hills never to be seen again.

Henry placed his glass on the chair arm, slowly stood and took the picture of his wife. Holding it close to his chest he began to weep for his dear wife, for whom he yearned more than words could ever say.

•••

Three miles north-east of Bath city centre in the county of Bath and North East Somerset lies a disused and abandoned airfield, which was used extensively for sorties out into the Channel during the second world war. It had lapsed into dereliction several years previously, being used consecutively as an Outward

Bound school, paintball gaming centre and washing machine storage facility. The local council had tried to sell it off for development but land survey engineers had detected substantial landslip possibilities and the project was shelved. The fact that it was in an area referred to as 'green belt' also gave any possible purchaser further problems as there were few exceptions to building in these designated 'green' areas. The airfield itself consisted of three corrugated iron aircraft hangars, all in varying degrees of dilapidation. Two had large holes in their roofs, and every one of them was without the sliding doors at each end and open to the elements. Refuse littered the floors, cider bottles and excrement mostly.

To the east was the control tower – or at least what was left of it. In the 80s a storm had hit the area, lightening had blown a hole in the supporting wall and over a period of time the elements and children using it for games of 'japs and commandoes' had done the rest. The runway would have been usable had gypsies not dug it up for the tarmac, leaving holes like a crazy-golf course along its length.

The only other building of consequence was the former armoury bunker and sometime washing machine storage facility. It differed from the hangars in that the sides and top of the building had been built up with soil. Grass grew freely and gave the bunker a look of permanency and the impression that it had always been part of the landscape. The other major difference was that it only had one set of sliding doors and they were still in good condition. Set inside the large sliding doors was a smaller hinged door for personnel to go in and out of and so negate the opening of the larger doors. Electricity had been cut off from the site several years ago, but ambient light from gas-powered lights seeped under the corrugated doors. Four cars were parked on the runway next to the bunker, all were top of their particular class except for a Ford Focus which had been stolen that very afternoon.

"What time do you make it?"

"Almost midnight. There is one other who should be here. No doubt he will leave it until the last possible moment," he sneered.

The six men standing in the bunker didn't know each other personally, except Nadeem and Jamal. But they did know each other by reputation and two of them had met by accident at one of the Taliban training camps in Afghanistan. Mustafa stood nearest the door waiting for Kamal. At one minute to twelve Mustafa heard a car approaching and stuck his head out through the door. He could see headlights coming down the track, bouncing erratically on the uneven earth. Stopping in a billow of dust the Corvette's door swung open and Kamal got out. As the assembled group hugged, kissed and congratulated each other, it was Mustafa who took charge and addressed the group.

"Why an American car?" asked Mustafa, distaste obvious in his question.

"It's the only good thing to ever come out of America," replied Kamal, smiling.

Mustafa laughed at the irony and turned to speak to the assembled group.

"You will forgive me if I say we are all here by royal appointment." He smiled as the others sniggered, appreciating his little joke. "We are the chosen ones, the few chosen to do our Saviour's bidding. We all received messages from Osama Bin Laden via his Al-Qaeda network to meet here tonight and receive our just rewards." Mustafa's voice went an octave higher and his eyes glowed with the fervour of the fanatic. "Our glorious leader has somehow managed to enter the United Kingdom and greet us personally. Should we be surprised? No! This is the same man who has outwitted and outsmarted the American vigilantes for years. They are no closer to finding him than they were four years ago. Tonight, we near the pinnacle of our plan. Each day we get closer to having a Muslim on the throne as King of England. We can rejoice, for surely we are the chosen faith."

"All praise to Allah," Mustafa shouted, whipping the small group up into a frenzy.

"All praise to Allah, All praise to—"

They at least died as they had lived, with Allah's name on their lips.

In each of the corners of the bunker was a fifty-gallon oil drum. Only they now held forty eight-gallons of unleaded petrol mixed with two-gallons of diesel fuel to help it stick. Taped to the inside of the drum was a cube of camera flashbulbs which were in turn linked to a single double-strand wire dug in, running north to the perimeter fence-line some hundred metres away. The solitary figure, dressed all in black, checked the Sony portable recorder and screen. The single camera high in the bunker's roof looked downwards; they were all, more or less, in the bunker's centre. He touched the bared wires to the 12-volt battery terminals and was rewarded by an enormous whooshing sound as all four drums exploded simultaneously, incinerating everyone inside. As an added measure, he had spent a whole day pulling washing machines that had been left behind up into the iron rafters, tying them off with ropes that now burned and dropped their heavy cargo down onto already lifeless bodies, crushing them completely.

Nothing like having a back-up plan. One is none and two is one.

Silently the figure walked the two miles back to his parked car, careful not to bump into anyone who might be walking their dog or up to some other unsavoury act.

•••

"Have you reached a verdict in which you all agree in respect of the case of the State of Florida versus Natalie Van Reissen?" asked the judge in the warm Tampa courtroom.

"We have, your Honour," answered the standing jury panellist.

"And what is your verdict?"

"We, the jury, find, in the case of the State of Florida versus Natalie Van Reissen in the first count of the first degree murder of John Swarovski… guilty. And in the second count of the first degree murder of Steven Jackson… guilty. And in the third count of the first degree murder of Richard Jackson… guilty, your Honour."

The assembled audience gasped as each of the verdicts was read out. No-one had really expected that the girl accused of these murders would be found guilty, especially under the circumstances that they had heard in court over the last five days.

Natalie put her head in her hands, disbelieving the verdict and unwilling to let the court see her cry.

Finally, after thanking the jury, the judge spoke.

"I have no other choice, given the circumstances and the verdict but to remand you to prison where, on the twelfth day of next month justice will be done and you will be given a lethal injection. May God have mercy on your soul." He banged his hammer. "Court is now closed."

The uproar in the courtroom was deafening as Natalie, handcuffed and wearing the usual orange overalls, was taken downstairs to the holding cells while waiting for transport to take her to the State Penitentiary. The press were clamouring for photographs and for her to give any kind of statement.

Natalie sat, stunned at the verdict, in her small barred cell. Her defence lawyer had done the best job he could but the odds were stacked against him from the start. It didn't help when the prosecution's star witness wheeled into the courtroom to give evidence against her.

Out of the nine men that had confronted her in that bedroom, three were dead from broken bones pushed into their heart and lungs. Two were on life support machines and never expected to ever lead a normal life again. Three had multiple breaks and contusions, one of those three would never have a sex life again. No-one would after having their dick ripped off and stuffed into their own mouth. That left Toby, the man who had organised and arranged the whole incident. It was he who was the man in the wheelchair. She'd laughed as she broke his legs and then his spine and he would remember that chilling sound for the rest of his life. Toby was a charismatic witness and gave a good, albeit slanted, view of the events. He maintained it was just a little fun and that Natalie had 'flipped' for no reason that he could make out. His recollections were substantiated by the others. All in all the lies lent credence to their stories and Natalie's version of events sounded hollow and untrue against the orchestrated prosecution evidence.

She was given leave to appeal but decided against doing so. She'd heard enough lies and felt that her life was now in the lap of the gods to do with as they wished, she couldn't know just how true that feeling was.

On the twelfth day Natalie was taken to the execution block. She refused a pre-med injection which the doctor had said would take the edge off the proceedings. She shuffled down the corridor, her legs shackled by a fourteen-inch chain. Even at the moment of her death they were determined to get their pound of flesh but Natalie held her head high; no longer would she be subjugated by anyone. Natalie's focus was on other things as she was laid on the table, slowly clearing her mind of discomfort. Thick leather straps fastened around her wrists, ankles and waist. They swabbed her arm and pushed in the catheter. Natalie thought it strange that they would use a disinfectant to cleanse her arm before inserting the needle. They wanted to kill her but not for her to get an infection – it all seemed ridiculous and surreal.

She was asked if she had any last words; she nodded and raised her head off the table, straining against the straps. She looked the small group of reporters in the eye and in a voice far too strong and confident she said simply and coldly.

"Fuck you all for letting this happen to me." then she lay back down awaiting the final tick of the clock at 3 p.m.

"Where am I?" she asked quietly of the dowdy man sitting in a chair next to her bed.

"You're in a private government-controlled secure hospital on the outskirts of London."

"I'm supposed to be dead."

"Yes, you are."

"Was it all a dream?"

"No. It was, unfortunately, all too real. To all intents and purposes you *are* dead."

Natalie sat up in the bed.

"Tell me everything and don't leave a single thing out." Her voice sounded far away and curious. There was no resentment, no anger.

"You were never going to get a fair trial in the United States. They couldn't allow a tourist to get away with killing two sons of a prominent congressman, no matter what the circumstances. I have looked into your case very closely. What you did was what anyone with your training would have done under those circumstances. Frankly, I admire your reserve at leaving anyone alive. Natalie, you have skills that very few people in this world will ever have. More importantly than the skills, you have a frame of mind that could be put to good use in cases of real injustice." He paused.

"Go on."

"Once you were pronounced dead we had thirty seconds to inject you with an antidote to the deadly serum. We switched bodies and had that other girl's medical documents switched as well so that they would match. You were brought into the UK in a coffin and you have been sleeping for thirty-two hours. I run an organisation that dispenses global justice to anyone or anything that threatens the United Kingdom and I want you to become a member of that organisation. The training will be difficult, near impossible. Very few have ever been offered a position in my organisation, let alone completed the training. You will be given a new face and a new identity and you will never find yourself in a courtroom ever again."

"I'll never be able to see my father nor any of my family will I?"

"No. I'm sorry. If you say yes, then that will be out of the question."

"And if I refuse? What will happen to me then?"

"As far as the world is concerned, you are already dead. Nothing will change," he said coldly. The man noticed her eyes were focused on the end of the bed as she absorbed what she'd been told.

"Do you need some time to think about it?" he asked gently.

"No. I will join your band of merry men under one condition." There was steel in her voice.

"What is it?" he asked, his curiosity piqued.

"Once I have completed the training and have my new face and identity, I want to return to the United States and ensure that the men who did this to me do not have the opportunity to do it to anyone else."

"Let us be clear. What you are saying is that once you are fully trained, you wish to kill the men who tried to rape you."

"Yes." Her voice was devoid of emotion yet full of certainty.

He stood up and offered his hand.

"Deal." She took his hand and shook it. Then the man went to leave the room.

"Regain your strength. In a few days we'll begin. Don't try to leave this room or you will be shot on sight. There are no second chances in this game, my dear."

Natalie nodded. She had no intention of leaving the room.

"Oh, one more thing. Each of my operatives is given a code name, usually a bird. I was thinking Sparrow-Hawk. How do you like it?"

"No." She shook her head. "I want to be called Phoenix." The name had come to her in an instant.

"Phoenix, huh. That's a mythical bird and not one I would have chosen."

"That may be, but the Phoenix rose from her ashes and destroyed those who would have destroyed her. I want that name," she said with a stubborn lilt of her chin.

The man stroked his chin.

"Then Phoenix it is."

"And speaking of names. What do I call you?" she asked as he reached the door. He turned and smiled.

"Director," he said affably, then he was gone.

●●●

He landed at Zurich International Airport an hour and twenty-five minutes after leaving Heathrow, less than three hours from detonating the deadly blast.

Mac had waited ten minutes for the Renaissance Hotel's transport but his impatience got the better of him and he walked down the ramp to the nearby taxi rank. Nine minutes later he'd filled in the requisite hotel form at reception and was now in room 425 on the fourth floor.

Leaving his small case on the bed, Mac wandered the hallways, checking for exit routes and obstacles. Satisfied, Mac returned to the room and went through each drawer until he found a copy of 'Die Gelben Seiten,' the Swiss equivalent of Yellow Pages.

On page 577 under 'Waffen' he noted three of the ten addresses. He'd look at these places tomorrow as he'd heard Switzerland had some unusual gun laws and thought he'd check them out.

Hanging up the clothes he would wear in the morning, Mac showered, then fell soundly asleep.

Waking at 7 a.m., Mac ordered breakfast via room service, showered again, shaved and was dressed just as he heard a knock at the door. Signing for breakfast Mac then called reception and arranged a taxi for thirty minutes, enough time to finish his meal then concentrate on the day's activities.

Exiting by the main doors the Mercedes E240 waited in the taxi bay. Sitting in the back Mac introduced himself and handed over a slip of paper on which were the three addresses. The driver, a native of Ghana who had lived in Switzerland for the last twelve years, took the paper and said he knew of these places. He spoke very good English and told Mac his birth name was Opoku.

The first location didn't open on Mondays, Wednesdays or Thursdays and was closed. The second, 'Waffen Galerie,' sold only ancient weapons, specialising in militaria, medals and a few swords. At the last location in Backerstrasse, Mac's curiosity was piqued as he spied an assault rifle in the window.

Expect that's an airsoft rifle, Mac thought. Meaning the six millimetre air powered weapons so favoured in the UK. With ever-increasing government restrictions on all types of firearms, the UK was foremost in the sale of these 'safe' plastic replicas.

Asking Opoku to wait, Mac entered the small shop and was astounded at the number of different automatic pistols on show. From early 1900 Brownings in 7.65 millimetre to brand new Sig-Sauer P229s and the large Desert Eagle in .45 calibre. This particular model was finished in burnished gold and looked like something that would grace the set of a Star Wars movie.

Mac waited his turn as the man at the counter purchased enough ammunition for a small country, or at least Yorkshire. Browsing further Mac noticed a current model Stg, the abbreviation meant 'Sturmgewehr', which was 'assault rifle' in English. It wasn't an airsoft after all but a semi-auto version of the military original.

Stumbling out of the store with his purchases, ammunition man barely made it to his Saab Aero before sustaining a coronary. To celebrate either the purchase of ammunition or having made it to the car without requiring major surgery, the man made his way to the nearest Keller and a cold beer.

Mac spoke quite good German from his years stationed in Dortmund and Hildesheim. It differed only a little from Swiss German.

"Do you have any nine millimetre blank fire flare pistols?" he asked, not having seen any amongst the other displayed goods.

"Yes, please, here." The elderly owner came from behind the counter and pulled a few boxes from a low display cabinet. There were several types of automatic pistol and one large magnum size revolver. Mac was looking for blank firing guns which were currently unavailable in the UK except with special Home Office approval and only as an eight millimetre Glock 17. France and Germany also no longer made them but, here and there, especially Spain and Italy, they could still be purchased without a licence.

Mac picked up a Berretta 94 Police issue model. There were two main types of blank firer, one that vented the blast upward and one that vented the blast forward, just like the real thing. They would come in useful for training exercises and disarm techniques. Mac didn't want any holes in the boat from using the real thing.

"How much?"

"You have a permit?"

"I need a permit to purchase a blank firer?" Mac asked, his voice raised an octave in astonishment.

"Yes, I'm sorry but you must have one," the storekeeper said apologetically.

"But for this one here, you don't need a permit." He showed Mac an identical model from a case.

"What's the difference?"

"For forward venting you must have a permit. For top venting, no permit is required."

"Ah," said Mac, now comprehending.

"This model and also the smaller one here are eight millimetre. Are they what you require?"

"Yes, thank you, I'll take both." Mac decided if only eight millimetre was available, he wouldn't quibble.

After paying three-hundred and sixteen Swiss Francs to the storekeeper, Mac took Opoku's mobile number and bade the driver take him to the Hauptbahnhof, Zurich's Main Railway Station.

Wandering around the sprawling train station Mac observed several things. One, there were no ticket barriers at any of the platforms nor could any inspector be seen. Two, there were hardly any closed-circuit video cameras. Three, there seemed to be a tranquil pace among the inhabitants and the station was devoid of the usual hustle and bustle normally associated with London stations.

Mac slowly walked the station's length before he saw what he had been looking for. A blue background and a white suitcase with a box around it along with a white key above: 'left luggage.'

Following the signs that took him to a lower floor, Mac couldn't fail to spot the blue lockers that adorned either side of the subterranean level. Checking the posted instructions, which were fortunately in German and English, Mac inserted a five Franc coin into locker 1475, checked there was nothing inside, re-locked and pulled the key free of its lock. This would suffice as Mac's DLB, his Dead Letter Box. Here he would instruct the Director to leave the goods.

In many European countries they've stopped using left luggage lockers for fear of terrorism. Glad to see there are still a few civilised countries around.

Re-tracing his steps, Mac crossed over the busy road and continued up Bahnhofstrasse, an area of expensive shops and private banks. The cost of purchasing or renting property here was reputed to be the highest in the world.

It wasn't long before he saw the shops that would fulfill his next requirements. Purchasing an LG 'Chocolate' phone and a small Nikon 5.5 mega-pixel camera with USB lead and appropriate software, Mac followed his nose and headed left through a wide ginnel that led him to an enclosed square. A small bistro at the far end served beer and sandwiches. At the grassed oblong area in the centre Mac placed the left luggage key on a bench alongside a five Franc coin and photographed both sides of the key close up. Once he'd finished he checked the photos on the viewer and when satisfied, went to the bistro, sat outside at a yellow-clothed table and ordered a club sandwich and fresh orange juice, no ice. The sun was warm but under the bistro's canopy Mac sat coolly, quite content.

I'm not sure if I like Switzerland or not. Sure it's clean, the people are polite, you hardly ever see a policeman but, it's… it's… characterless, boring? Yes, that's it, there's hardly any personality to the place.

Mac sat ruminating.

I'd probably fit right in.

•••

"Are we any further?"

"No, Director, I'm sorry. The information so far is that seven men of Asian or Arabic origin were killed by an, as yet, unidentified explosion."

"Has there been any word from Shrike?" The Director, once an avid bird watcher, had given bird names to each of the operatives, at the same time unconsciously apportioning each bird's abilities to how he viewed each operative. Mac was 'Shrike,' a bird that lured other birds into barbed obstacles. Once they had exhausted themselves by trying to get out of the trap, the Shrike would tear them to pieces and eat them.

"None. He's missed his monthly check-in but with him, that's not altogether unusual. He usually surfaces, and there have been several occasions when his check-in schedule has been missed by far more than six days."

"Humph." Henry wasn't convinced.

"Security is still on high alert for the remaining Royals but there haven't been any more attacks, not a peep. Funny that... what?"

"I'll send messages to the operatives, give them an update and see if there's anything they can add," Helen said, poised with pen for instructions.

"Yes," said Henry distantly.

It just didn't add up and if there was one thing Henry Bishop hated, it was anomalies.

Fifteen minutes after Helen and the Director had their meeting, an email arrived in Helen's tray. She read it quickly then downloaded the attachments which appeared to be two photographs of a key next to a coin. The message read....

AT 1600 HOURS TOMORROW (FRIDAY) SECURE
COMMUNICATIONS
CACHED IN 1475 ZURICH HAUPTBAHNHOF.
NO OTHER FORM OF DEBRIEF ACCEPTABLE.
DEATH OF LADY DI AND OSAMA BIN LADEN
CONNECTED.
BET I HAVE YOUR ATTENTION NOW.

Helen entered Henry's office without preamble or knocking.
"Sir, I think you should read this."
Henry took the offered pages.
"Death of Lady Di and Osama Bin Laden connected? What on earth could one have to do with the other? Who's it from?"
"Shrike, sir."

Henry sat back in his chair.

"Shrike? So, we have to take this information seriously and, judging by the request for secure communications, so does he."

"You'll forgive me, Director but what does the message mean and why photos of a key?"

"One four seven five and Zurich Hauptbahnhof denote a left luggage locker in the city's main train station. The photos are of the key to that locker."

"And the coin?"

"To give us scale. The coin is a known and documented quantity, from that we can work out the key's measurements. We'll need a key to be able to leave the equipment and Shrike will need his key to retrieve it."

"Oh. Clever isn't he." Helen remarked as she left Henry's office.

"Yes," said the Director looking at the photos.

"A right clever little bastard."

•••

An hour after the goods should have been left, Mac stood watching at the far side of the subterranean level as Gretchen opened the door to locker 1475 and withdrew a small silver handset.

He looked up and down at the few who were dotted around the area. An elderly couple walking hand in hand, obviously still very much in love judging by the looks and smiles they gave each other. A group of three female teenagers heading to the escalators, chattering loudly in a similar volume to their outlandish clothing. The remaining candidate, a solitary thirty-something male reading instructions on a notice board. He was relaxed, showing no physical signs of the surveillance operative, absorbed as he was in the warning notices. No tension, no sideways glances or words mouthed into hidden microphones.

Gretchen stepped onto the upward escalator, Mac a discreet distance behind her. He gave the impression he was completely at ease but his slow studied gaze missed nothing. Unaware she was being shadowed, Gretchen made her way to the corner cafe as Mac moved at right angles to her direction, again studying the stations inhabitants.

So far, nothing. Good. Glad they've seen sense.

Mac waited at the newsagents stand leafing through a copy of 'Stuff': a magazine dedicated to the latest in electronics and machines. There were no signs that either he or Gretchen were being watched. Purchasing an edition of The Wall Street Journal, Mac unhurriedly made his way to the cafe and sat opposite Gretchen at a small round table.

"Very good," Mac complimented her.

"You're a natural." he added.

"Thank you, it was fun." Suddenly conspiratorial, she leaned over her hot chocolate. "Was I being followed?"

"Yes." Mac lied, then leaned forward also.

"The two men reading newspapers to your right, don't look, and the lady in the blue frock near platform four are ex-KGB. Once you pass me the radio guidance chip in this newspaper, they'll follow me and I'll lose them." Mac placed the journal on the table. Gretchen pulled out the silver handset, slipped it in the newspaper and folded it.

"But it looks like a mobile phone?" she asked, expecting an explanation. She wasn't disappointed.

"Ah yes, that's the point. It looks like a mobile phone. They couldn't just leave behind a small guidance chip in the locker. They disguised it to look like something that everyone carries. Clever chaps aren't they." Mac winked.

Gretchen had been with a group of students home from their boarding days at a private school near Basel, all dressed in the school colours of light blue skirts and white blouses. Mac had noticed that while the group were animated in recounting what they had been up to during the sojourn in rapid-fire German, she was quiet and vulnerable, slightly apart from the majority. He'd approached her anxiously, explaining he was with British Military Intelligence, pushed a 1000 Swiss Franc into her hand and quickly gave her instructions as to what she needed from her. Mac's warmth and feigned anxiousness worked wonders, he had engaged her curiosity.

There are many types of people who love a good conspiracy but none more than the Germans. They even have a word for it 'Geheimnes.'

Without giving her time to think it over, Mac steered her towards the top escalator.

"Do this for your country," said Mac as he'd walked away in the opposite direction.

Gretchen was seventeen, tall, blonde and with a high I.Q. She'd spent a whole week with her estranged parents who each lived in separate parts of the schloss and each with separate lives. She'd been bored to tears. Now, presented with a little adventure, how could she possibly say no.

Mac watched from a distance as she descended into the lower level.

Good girl.

"I'll lead them away. You go and stand with your friends."

Gretchen placed her hand on top of Mac's.

"Is there anything else I can do for you? My train doesn't leave for another twenty-five minutes." she said invitingly.

Mac shook his head wistfully.

"Another time little Gretchen… another time. I must leave now."

"Wait. Here is my number." She handed over a serviette with numbers written on it in eyeliner. Mac took it then kissed her on the forehead.

"Goodbye, dear Gretchen, auf wiedersehen."

Mac swiftly left the cafe. Gretchen waited twenty seconds then married up with the waiting ensemble, now smiling enigmatically; it wasn't long before others noticed and she became the centre of attention. The girls clustered around her, listening enviously as she recounted a rather more embellished version of her mini-adventure.

chapter nineteen

Mac strode purposefully towards Bahnhofstrasse then weaved his way through the smaller alleyways and narrow streets until he felt comfortable and reassured that he could not possibly have been followed.

I'll keep moving. It could well be that there is a tracking device in the phone. I don't really think there will be but I need to cover every base.

Taking an abrupt detour through the stationery store 'Zumstein,' Mac stood in a nearby doorway, half watching for a tail and half looking at the silver phone.

It's one of the twenty-four bit encrypted phones sold by Tripleton. I remember seeing them on the internet at 'Tripleton.co.uk'. They use military grade cyphers, considered to be unbreakable.

Mac pressed the 'on' button, checked it had a good strong four bar signal then checked the 'contacts' folder. In it was a single UK number already annotated with the UK country code of 00 44. Mac had read about the encrypted phone in 'Eye Spy,' a UK-based magazine giving updates on global terrorism and surveillance technology.

Each phone has to be given a cypher from the phone that it wants to call. If each phone has not been programmed with the receiving cypher then it can't de-crypt the signal it's receiving... neat.

Mac closed his eyes for an instant, gathering his thoughts as he recalled everything he needed to pass on and everything he needed to say.

He pressed 'call'.

The phone was answered on the first ring.

"Shrike?" came the excited urgent question.
"You're recording this?" came the cool rejoinder.
"Yes." said the Director, changing back to his normal less-than-excited self.
"Good. Because I don't want to have to repeat myself and I don't want there to be any misunderstanding about what I'm about to say."

The director felt a sense of foreboding and disquiet but kept it from the timbre of his reply.
"Go ahead."
"Before I proceed I want it understood there will be no questions until I ask for them. Ok?"
"Understood, Shrike. Go ahead, please."
Mac took a deep breath and began.
"As you are aware, I was contracted by the Lebanese government to persuade Osama Bin Laden to retire. If he refused, I was to retire him myself. This was in exchange for a three billion dollar influx of funds to help Lebanon move ahead into the twenty-first century."

The Director couldn't help himself.
"Yes yes, get to the…"
Mac cut in, his voice colder than Alaska on a December night.
"If you interrupt once more, I'll switch this phone off and you can spend the rest of your life guessing what I'm about to say."
Mac's phone remained quiet, the Director, suitably chastised.
"As I was saying," Mac continued.
"I found the real Al-Zarqawi in an American rendition camp in Lesotho. The Al-Zarqawi that everyone is chasing is a decoy, a Jordanian citizen blackmailed into posing as the wanted man. He was near death when I got to him. During the escape he was shot but before he died gave me the location of where he believed Osama was hiding. The co-ordinates led me to the mountains near a village in El Salvador just short of the Honduran border. There I

found a subterranean complex filled with computers." Mac paused. The Director wasn't so foolish as to interrupt twice.

"The computers were maintained by an undisclosed American agency. They had been in place since 1995, sifting through emails and telephone conversations distilled from Echelon and Mercury and God knows how many other sources. The computers received original instructions from an unidentified source and I believe these instructions were meant to de-stabilise global democracies and governments."

Mac continued to walk steadily through the back roads and alleyways of the world's private banking capital.

"You had asked me to look out for any information relating to the assassinations of Royal Family members. The details to that operation came via the computers in El Salvador. A team of seven men were trained, paid and organised to kill directly on orders from these computers. It would seem to me that the idea was to de-stabilise the United Kingdom by putting a Muslim on the throne as King of England."

Henry gasped so loud that Mac heard it and chuckled to himself.

I knew that would grip him by the short and curlies. Wait till he gets the rest!

"Princess Diana had a male child by Dodi Fayed. It was kept a secret but someone found out. Diana and Dodi were killed and it was made to look like an accident. The child, only months old, was abducted and brought up in the Islamic faith. He now lives in Qatar but I don't know where or what he is now called."

"You're sure of this?" Henry blurted, no longer able to contain himself.

Mac said nothing for ten seconds then continued, disregarding Henry's outburst.

"By adding commands to the computer's main program code, I sent seven terrorists to a disused airbase in Somerset. Once they were together, I killed them all. No doubt you have already had a report on this event? No further assassinations will take place. The Royal line of succession is safe."

"Thank God." whispered Henry.

"Now. This is where it really gets interesting... Osama Bin Laden is dead."

"What! You killed him?"

Mac decided it was better to let the Director ask his questions before he keeled over with frustration.

"No, I didn't kill him. He died in a landfall, a mountain climbing accident in the Afghan mountains six years ago." Mac let the information sink into the Directors brain.

"Six years... that's impossible... I mean... six years... SIX YEARS!"

He's got it now.

"You've verified this?" The director's head hurt with the ramifications.

"Yup. One hundred and ten percent. What you've got to figure is... If Osama Bin Laden died six years ago..."

"...who organised the 9/11 disaster and who's been making the videos of him since?" The Director finished the thought-provoking question.

"My point entirely. With the evidence I've seen, it would seem that it was all arranged by the Americans themselves."

"What!"

"Hear me out. I don't have a shred of hard proof. It's all been destroyed but I have read it with my own eyes. The American people were becoming extremely disgruntled with their government. The White House's policies were in disarray and the President's popularity was at an all time low. Suddenly, out of nowhere a large well-organised invisible group of Islamic extremists appear, hijack several planes and smash them into American buildings on American soil. Coincidence? I don't think so. Then the government is galvanised into action. Security is deemed paramount, many companies with ties to the President's family get awarded multi-million dollar contracts to preserve American security and the American psyche. By demonstrating to the public just how vulnerable they are, they've signed away a lot of their freedom. The government has now, with the invasion of Iraq, ensured a plentiful supply of enemies. And, many American companies are making billions of dollars selling security and peace of mind to its unwitting citizens."

"Do you really think the President of the United States is behind all this?"

"No. Not him directly but some offshoot of one select committee or agency knows what's going on even if the President doesn't."

"It beggars belief," said Henry with a tinge of exhaustion to his voice.

"One other thing that beggars belief." Mac added.

"There's more?"

"I'm retiring, leaving, finished, I'm not working for you or anyone any more."

"Now just a momen…"

"No! You've had more than a moment, you've had my life. Now I'm taking it back. When I said I didn't have proof, I lied. Anything, and I mean anything happens to me, the information gets released simultaneously on four continents. It would be in everyone's interests to forget about me. So, here's the deal. You leave me alone and I'll leave you."

"But what…" The phone clicked dead.

"He's switched it off. I can't believe it, he's switched it off?" said Henry to the desk blotter and himself.

After switching off the phone Mac walked over to an open-topped Ferrari parked outside an antique shop and dropped the phone behind the passenger seat.

If there is a tracking device, they can follow these two.

The middle-aged driver and his pigtailed pre-pubescent girlfriend came out of the shop carrying an eighteenth-century cuckoo clock.

It's Switzerland… what else would you buy?

Mac smiled as he realised he was free to do as he pleased, then became morose as he remembered that he didn't have anyone to share that freedom with.

I can always buy a cuckoo clock.

He laughed to himself but it didn't make him feel any better.

chapter twenty

Sitting in the back of the air-conditioned airport taxi, Mac wondered at the incongruities of Hong Kong life.
Their maxim is 'one country, two systems.' Now that Hong Kong is once again part of China not much seems to have changed. At least the Chinese government has been smart enough not to tamper with the business status quo. Colonialism still runs very deep, they haven't even changed the road signs, they're still in Chinese and English and they still drive on the British side of the road.
The yellow cab came to a rest at Aberdeen Marina, currently managed by Shangri-La International. Mac paid the driver and turned to the security gate where the guard, resplendent in a pale blue uniform and slashed peak cap, ensured his name was verified on the daily admittance sheet. Once the guard confirmed Mac's name was on the list he flung a salute worthy of a Coldstream Guardsman and bade Mac enter the secure docking area.
Mac had called ahead from the UK giving Manny his flight number and arrival time. He could see his boat on pier six, Mac felt a genuine affection for the craft and relaxed his shoulders; he was coming 'home.' The Sicilian Princess was the second largest boat currently moored and as such was regarded by many as an object of envy. The marina security commander had been surprised that after mooring for five days he had not seen the owner but such was the lives of men who could afford to purchase and run such a magnificent vessel. Consequently he had made subtle enquiries as to the owner's identity, getting only as far as a registered company in the Seychelles.

About twenty percent of the marina around the Sicilian Princess was undergoing re-construction. Indonesian and Malay workers swarmed over the site like over-active ants. Mac carried only an overnight bag, he'd been too impatient to wait for luggage to be offloaded, so travelled light.

Everything I need is on the boat... well, almost everything.

The boat looked in tip-top condition. The four-man crew were just disembarking which struck Mac as curious.

Maybe they're coming to greet me?

Manny fronted the boisterous group who waved at Mac and walked towards him. As they drew level Manny shook Mac's hand warmly; the others crowded round Mac patting him on the back and shoulders in a congratulatory manner, talking rapidly but warmly in an unintelligible Greek dialect. Manny continued to shake Mac's hand vigorously, while waving the others away; soon they were alone.

"Heed my words," he said enigmatically, "you take good care of her and she'll take care of you."

It seemed obvious Manny was referring to the gleaming boat.

"I will," Mac said sincerely.

"Good, good." Manny went to catch up with the others.

"Where you going?" Mac shouted after him.

"For a well earned bottle of Ouzo, maybe two. We'll be back later, give you some time to... re-adjust. Don't forget what I said," he shouted back, cupping his hand to his mouth. Several Malay workers turned at the noise then jabbered to each other for ten seconds or so as they realised they weren't in trouble.

Mac shrugged his shoulders and shook his head as he headed up the gang-plank eager for the air-conditioned main deck. He stopped for an instant, then turned, his sixth sense alert.

I can feel it. Someone's watching me...

Mac scanned the near ground then the buildings further away.

...naw, you're just getting paranoid in your old age. Come on, let's enjoy our retirement, forget all this shit.

Mac laughed out loud. He was glad to be back. Mac had never felt safe staying in one place for too long. With the Sunseeker being registered under a Seychelles company and the use of nominee directors, there was little chance of anyone making the connection between him and the immaculate vessel. Turning left along the side and onto the wood panelled floor of the stern dining area, he was smiling to himself, happy that the mission was completed and that a long relaxing period loomed ahead.

Music slowly filtered through his veil of contentment, Mac was momentarily confused.

The music's coming from inside the main salon? Who the...?

The realisation suddenly hit home. Mac dropped his overnight bag and took a step back from the salon doors as though hit by an electrical charge.

Shit!

Through the wood and stained glass doors Mac could easily make out the words to the song, the solitary piano accompaniment and strong male voice boomed from the Bang and Olufsen speakers. He recognised the tones of Lionel Ritchie and the song title, 'Truly'.

Boy; tell me only this, that I have your heart
For always, and, you want me by your side
Whispering the words "I'll always love you,"

And forever, I will be your lover
And I know that you really care
I will always; be there.

Mac's pulse raced with a surge of adrenaline. He'd rather face a room full of terrorists or the criminally insane rather than go inside and face whatever was waiting for him behind those doors.

I need to tell you this, there's no other love, like your love,
And, as long as I live, I'll give you all the joy
My heart and soul can give....

Taking deep breaths Mac steadied his pulse, settled his nerves, cricked his neck then opened the salon doors and strode through with more confidence than he really felt.

Becky was on the leather settee at the far end of the salon, sitting cross-legged, skirt riding up to her thighs, Scooby held to her chest with one hand, the other dabbing at her puffy eyes swollen with constant crying. She looked up at Mac then deliberately put down the tissue, picked up the remote control and muted the CD player.

Mac stopped dead as though an invisible force field held him at bay.

This was what Manny was referring to, not the boat – am I stupid or what?

"Becky I..."

She quickly held up her hand silencing further comment then she kissed Scooby on the nose and seated him, surrounded by cushions. She glided from the settee, composed, in control.

Mac adopted the open-on-all-eight-sides position, feet shoulders-width apart, toes slightly out-turned, knees casually bent. Hands loose at his sides, elbows tucked in, palms out-turned, fingers relaxed, ready to react to any situation. In the six years Becky had been training she hadn't yet reached this level of readiness and had never been taught this stance.

Mac noticed she was wearing a loose bottle-green sleeveless top with alternating sequins in a V-shape between her breasts. A matching crinkly skirt with ragged light green lace at the hem gave her the appearance of young gypsy girl. She was barefoot. Mac also noticed that her hands were devoid of weapons but with Becky that didn't really count for much.

Mac had never seen her so fluid, so graceful in her movements. It was like she was floating.

She glides, like death on skates.

Becky crossed the twenty feet between them silently, her eyes focused on Mac's, unwavering.

She could be so pissed off with me that we'll end up fighting, or, she's come to tell me that she's glad to be rid of me. That she's upset but she'll get over it.

At six feet away Becky stopped and put her hand behind her back, Mac emptied his mind, he was as ready as he'll ever be.

Becky's hand slowly came back into view, in it was a single sheet of paper, Mac's letter.

"What's the meaning of this?" she asked, her tone quiet and all the more chilling for it.

"I…"

"Be quiet! I talk, you listen, got it?" Her voice took on an edge. It was the same edge that Mac would sometimes take with her.

"We've known each other for, how long now?" Her gaze held steady. Mac knew how a water buffalo felt when trapped by a tiger, he didn't answer, he wasn't meant to.

"Six years. In that time I've learned so much. Control, breathing, technique. What it's like to take someone's life, what it's like to feel truly alive. What have you learned?"

Mac had never heard Becky so eloquent, decisive. He waited some more.

"I'm not sure what you've learned. But I know what you haven't." Becky paused.

Whatever's going to happen, it's going to happen now.

"For a man so academically brilliant, so resourceful, you can be quite thick you know. God, you haven't a clue have you? Don't you realise? It doesn't matter how many times I get shot. It doesn't matter how many near death experiences I have. Nothing matters except…" Becky covered the remaining distance between them startlingly fast, her hands moved quickly towards his neck.

I can't, won't stop her. If this is to be the way it ends, so be it.

Mac tensed awaiting the killer blow.

It never came. It was replaced with her mouth hungrily seeking his, her hands continued forward encircling his head, pulling him towards her. Becky's body moulded itself against him. Momentarily stunned, Mac ultimately responded. The barriers he'd put in place between them came crashing down like the twin towers of 9/11.

She was everything he thought she'd be, warm, vibrant, sensual, demanding, loving. He returned her passion then surprised them both by pulling free.

"Becky, Becky, please. I don't want to lose what we already have, our friendship, our…"

Becky placed her finger on Mac's lips. "Sshh. We'll still have our friendship. It's just…" Her eyes widened. "We'll have so much more as well."

"What about our age difference? Our lifestyle, what we do, what we've done. Don't you see that as a problem?"

Becky was undaunted.

"Do you?"

Mac paused a millisecond.

"No."

"Neither do I."

Becky took Mac's hand.

"Come with me," she said, gently pulling Mac in the direction of the owner's bedroom. After three paces she stopped and turned.

"Oh," she said casually, "two things. What do you call the stance you adopted?"

Mac was taken aback that she had noticed but hid his surprise well.

"Open-on-all-eight-sides, made famous by Miyamoto Musashi, the legendary twin-bladed swordsman," he answered without guile.

"What's the other thing?"

Becky smiled, Mac saw her face cloud and her demeanour change. Soothingly, almost sibilantly she replied.

"If you ever do this to me again," she stroked his lapels lovingly and whispered softly, "I'll kill you."

Mac heard the same words he'd used with the Director over eight months ago. He meant it then as surely as she meant it now. His response echoed the Director's.

"I know." Mac's voice was thick with emotion.

"Come on. We've got a lot of catching up to do," she giggled, her mood abruptly changing once again, grasping his hand.

"Hold on, just a minute. How did you find me?"

Becky froze then answered sheepishly not meeting Mac's eyes.

"I memorised the boat's transponder frequency, had a friend hack into the World Maritime Locator Chart website and voila, here I am."

"You memorised the transponder frequency? Why?"

"Just in case you ever tried to leave me," she added hesitantly as if guilty of some cardinal sin.

Mac shook his head. "You never cease to amaze me."

She leant forward and whispered into Mac's ear.

"Come with me and I'll amaze you some more."

As Becky guided Mac to the bedroom door he stole a glance through the portal, noticing a construction sign on the marina walkway. Somehow, it seemed to sum up everything in a way that he never could.

White letters on a red background, it read... 'DANGER AHEAD.'

epilogue

The Director sat contemplatively at the twin-terminaled computer desk considering his next move carefully. After nearly an hour he typed instructions to Stork and Phoenix then emailed them using a sophisticated encryption program. He had finally made up his mind. Even though it broke protocol he was going to unite two members of Action Six. It was the norm that none of the operatives ever met but he considered that no single agent would be capable of finding Mac let alone getting the information off him.

Desperate times call for desperate measures. Shrike cannot be trusted to keep the information he says he has. I don't believe he would use it but if anything happened to him, an accident or plain ill health he may not be able to send whatever messages he needs to stop the information being released by whoever is holding it. The emails I've sent instruct Stork and Phoenix to find Shrike and get the information off him at all costs. They are like chalk and cheese and I'm hoping that between them they can come up with a winning strategy. They know he used to be one of my operatives and I've advised them to be extremely careful. Shrike cannot and should not be under-estimated.

Once the emails had been sent, Henry felt a wave of exhaustion overcome him and for the first time he could remember in a long time, he put on his hat and coat and left the office voluntarily.

Helen, sitting in the reception area was so startled to see the Director finish early she almost said something inappropriate.

He looks so tired. This last three weeks really have taken their toll.

∙∙∙

He'd been here two days before she arrived. Once again his friend had helped, this time a full background check had revealed many things. The most notable and immediately useful was the flight reservation to Hong Kong. The remainder beggared belief.

This young girl's description, or something close to it, was on seven of the world's intelligence databases. It said she was sometimes in the company of a much older man but little else. Her description was linked to a dozen murders and other incidents, all of them without the slightest shred of hard evidence. Sometimes it was no more than she was in the same country at the time of some incident. I'll really have to research the full report when I get back.

His physical reserves were running low, the pro-plus and two Red Bulls for breakfast helped, not only physically but psychologically too.

She arrived looking fresh but now he saw her in a different light, no longer the little girl. She was too good to be anything but professionally trained. He knew when the plane would land and had as much as possible prepared. The last of his funds had been used on the Sony video camera with digital zoom of x 800 and the waiting taxi, its meter ticking over for almost thirty minutes already.

He cursed himself for his stupidity at underestimating her, something he had been trained specifically not to do, he wouldn't do it again.

She'd hailed a cab and he'd followed her to the marina, he wasn't going to risk trying to get past the security guard but did manage to find himself a good vantage point on the top floor of a nearby building under construction.

It's all there if you have the eyes to see. The compact movements, the fluidity, her awareness masked by her beauty and youth. Christ she's good. Why she left me alive I'll never understand but then, that's her mistake.

He'd waited overnight, his hunger diminished by Mars Bars and a bottle of Coke, his training kicking in.

Wish I had a pound for every hour I've spent on stag observing, waiting for that one specific photograph, that one specific person. All the cold months sat in bushes in County Fermanagh and Armagh. Belfast was a doddle by comparison.

Once he'd finished the drink it doubled as a piss bottle. Don screwed the top on tight, he didn't want his own urine spilling inside his pocket and down his leg.

There was little activity on the Sunseeker. Now and again a male crewmember would wander from the cockpit, walk around for a while then go back inside. He never saw the girl again.

Late in the morning a lone male entered the marina and headed for the moored boat. Don videoed him.

Doesn't seem like anyone special. Just a little short-arse geezer. Wait a minute...

As Don continued to zoom in and record, Manny and the other three crew left the boat and wandered in the stranger's direction. As they drew level they seemed to be congratulating him then they left the marina and the lone figure appeared confused.

He looks like any other fifty something male but... It's the way he walks, the deliberate unhurried calculated movements, the way he moved up the undulating gangplank still completely balanced.

It suddenly dawned on him.

She hasn't taught him, he's taught her. Wait... he's stopped... looking around at possible observation points. He's got a predator's senses. Christ, it's as though he can see me even though I know he can't.

Don shuddered involuntarily.

This is him. This is the man who pulled the trigger on the Prime Minister, I know it.

Don checked his watch.

Bollocks. I've got to get to the airport and catch my flight back to the UK. If I had any money left I'd stay and have a chat with the guy, but I can wait. Guru didn't die for nothing. Now I know where you are, the name of your girl and the name of the boat. I'll find you again... count on it.

Don didn't have any money left for a taxi and it was a long walk back to Lantau airport but he didn't mind.

Luck's been shitting on me all year but now, now it's changed. I'll be back, then we'll see...then we'll fuckin' see.

six weeks later

The wooden floored dojo was empty save for a diminutive figure dressed in a stark white karate gi slashed in half with a belt of black. It is a well-believed myth that by reaching the status of a black belt, you are at the top of the martial arts class. The truly enlightened know that this is but another stage in the search for the perfection of technique and a state of openness referred to as no-mind.

No-mind is a state of readiness, without being ready. A place where you do not react to threats but act to precipitate them or, in your perfection, do not allow the threat to ever materialise in the first instance. Your movements are without thought and thus swift to the point of being almost uncanny. We have all at some time or other experienced no-mind but we probably didn't even realise it. That little bit of intuition that tells us to slow down at the street corner and as we do, we miss bumping into the person coming in the opposite direction. When we are in a kitchen or at work and we accidentally brush against something, a stapler, a fork. We knock it from the counter and then, without thinking, we catch it in our left hand instead of our right. Action without thought, this is no-mind.

The slender figure moved her left foot forward slowly and pressed her toes into the worn floor surface adopting the Cat-Foot-Stance. Her right hand, open, palm upward at her hip and her left hand relaxed, with fingers lightly curled, bent at the elbow in front of her ready to ward off imaginary blows.

Spinning on her heel and toes she turned 180 degrees and moved both hands level with her large breasts, palms out and fingers bent into claws.

WHOOSH!

The first tennis ball came hurtling towards her at seventy-miles per-hour. She turned to her left and swung with her right hand, hitting the yellow ball mid-flight, sending it towards the green mats used for judo.

As part of the blocking technique she widened her stance and lowered her body so as to make a smaller target. She continued with her kata, a sequence of movements that must be executed with perfect timing. Pushing both hands up to the sky and keeping her breathing regular she slowly brought her hands down to her hips and clenched them.

WHOOSH!

The second ball came hurtling towards her from a different direction. Diving forward in an arc she took the roll across her back and came up with a rolling-block along her left forearm, hitting the ball before it could connect with any major part of her body. The yellow menace careered off into the far corner, bouncing from the wall and into a suspended punch-bag.

Moving from her original Wado-ryu kata and into Gojushiho Dai, one of the more difficult Shotokan katas. She was at the point of the Rising Elbow Strike with her right hand almost behind her neck and her elbow thrust upwards when she heard the third and last of the CO_2 powered tennis ball shooters. This was the fastest of the three and shot a ball at over 85 miles per hour, directly at her upper body. At only twenty-five feet away Natalie Van Reissen had less than a quarter of a second to decide what to do. She decided not to decide. Once a course of action is chosen then you are limited to that course; by not choosing a course of action, her possibilities were limitless.

It was as if time stood still for her. She saw everything. The ball coming towards her. The distance from her to the projectile and lastly her own hand, which plucked the ball from mid-air. She caught it without a single thought, No-mind.

After a rigorous workout Natalie showered. At five-foot two, she was small and her body was hard with compact muscle from the training she'd received in dojos like this and in Japan. The long selection and training course the Director had subjected her to had also gone a long way to sculpting her physique.

That course had been the hardest thing I've ever done. Even more arduous than my year in Japan with the masters.

There was no-one else in the dojo, she'd booked it for her exclusive use, two hours each morning from 9am to 11am, three days a week.

The tennis ball machines were a good idea. I can set the timers for up to one hour and by looking away when I spin the timer I've no idea when it will go off.

Natalie had got the idea after reading a comic book about the X-men, a Marvel Comics creation. The Superheroes would train in a holographic chamber labelled 'The Danger-Room'. Threats would materialise and the superhero group would have to react to each threat as it happened, without ever knowing what would occur. This was Natalie's version, albeit less interesting or threatening than a twenty-foot robot or radioactive spider, it would tune her senses to unexpected danger and sharpen her reflexes.

I don't like to include anyone in my workout. I have difficulty in pulling back and not following through with the technique. It's got to the stage where I could seriously hurt someone I'm sparring with and I wouldn't want to hurt an innocent.

Natalie's phone rang, ending the review of her training. She carried two phones. One for day-to-day use and this one, for business.

"Hello?"

"Hello, my dear." came the cultured tones of Kensington Dalyrimple-Plantagenet. "We have a lead and by all accounts it's a very good one. Shall we say, the usual place at two?"

"Yes. See you there." The phone went dead.

A lead? Another one? They're all supposed to be good leads and where has it got us, nowhere. Wherever you are, Mister Machiavelli, you've done a brilliant job of hiding but time is on our side and sooner or later we'll get lucky and then we'll find you.

She smiled a secret smile.

I'm really looking forward to it.

...to be continued

Mac and Becky's adventures continue in...

The Mutuus Protocol

Her breathing was rapid and she was sweating profusely with the effort of running up the steep hill. It didn't help that the path was narrow, overgrown and in some places treacherous to a misplaced foot.

Keep going. Forget the stitch in your side and the taste of blood in your mouth. It's just your body telling you to quit... no way.

The high leg combat boots were heavy and hindered her getting into a proper stride but they were necessary to stop her legs and feet from being scratched or bitten by the hundred-million or more insects that she would encounter during her training run. She was two miles from the house and a twisted ankle or worse could cause quite a problem in this terrain as she'd left any communication devices at the place she now called home.

I remember my first time in a jungle in Lesotho. It really took it out of me, both physically and mentally. I don't want that to happen again. Not that we are in that kind of life any more... yeah right. Something will happen, it always does.

Becky watched where she placed her feet, a few inches to the right or left and she'd slip over the steep ridgeline. Hardly life threatening but it kept her mind sharp all the same.

Just over this false stone ridge then another hundred metres and I'll be at the top... about time!

Without slowing her fast steady pace Becky surmounted the final ridge and stood proudly at the top. Checking her watch she found she was four seconds slower than the last time she did this route two weeks ago.

Drat!!

She often varied her route, not out of a change of routine to foil the bad guys, she just liked a change of scenery now and again.

The view is marvellous! All that lush greenery teeming with life...

She was quite still for a moment as the irony of the situation suddenly hit her.

...much like myself eh?

"Hi," came a voice that startled her. Becky turned. Her senses immediately alert.

"Hi yourself," Becky was surprised to see a young girl, slight and smaller than herself standing in a relaxed pose almost twenty-feet away, there was something about her stance, it reminded Becky of a rubber band; taught and ready to snap, even though she was obviously very much in control of herself. As her sixth sense and situation awareness kicked in Becky realised she was not facing a lost tourist or rambler but an adversary.

Admittedly she caught me unawares but she lost that advantage by warning me of her presence. What's she up to? Anyway, as Mac would say 'take the initiative' or one of his many sayings like ' the way of a samurai is one of immediacy.' Or something like that.

"So how do we do this?" she asked with a smile.

Hell! She recovered quickly. I thought I might have shaken her a little by appearing like that. This is going to be a good contest, I can tell that already.

"How about if I throw the first punch?" Natalie wasn't about to be wrong footed so easily.

Becky shrugged. "Ok."

Natalie was in a loose fitting light green tracksuit, her long hair pulled back into a pony-tail, she'd dressed for the occasion ensuring her clothes were fitted but not restrictive. Moving towards Becky, ready for whatever would occur.

"Wait!" Becky held up her hand. "Before we begin I need to know if your prepared to kill me or not." The question threw Natalie, she stopped and raised her eyebrows at the unusual question.

"No. I need to take you hostage and at the same time I was curious as to just how good you are." Becky pondered the answer for a moment.

"If you're here to separate me from Mac and use me as leverage, well, it just won't work."

Wow! She's quick. She deduced all that in an instant. She's insightful and dangerous... good.

"We'll see."

"Yes, we will."

Natalie moved forward in a fencer's stance, moving her front foot forward then pulling in her rear foot quickly so as to keep her balance and readiness. She needn't have bothered. Becky caught her with a low kick to her shin when she was still two steps away. Natalie recovered and threw a knife-hand strike to Becky's temple, it almost made contact but was blocked. Becky moved closer and whipped up her elbow, expecting it to connect with the girls chin, it only hit the humid jungle air. They each took a step back and circled.

"You're faster than I thought you'd be," said Natalie with grudging admiration.

Becky stayed silent.

Anyone else and this fight would already be over. The low kick followed by a high elbow strike has never failed, there's more to her than meets the eye. She's more skilful than I am but I remember Mac telling me that not every confrontation is a matter of skill. In this instance he's definitely right.

Natalie took the initiative this time, her low, middle then high kick combination finally caught Becky on the cheek, she reeled back under the powerful blow. Natalie kept up the pressure and dropped to the ground hitting Becky with a low leg sweep. Becky fell but managed to roll away as she regained her feet Natalie was on her again. Becky's intense training with Mac had prepared her for any engagement but this was something else and it was only her razor sharp reflexes that saved her from being knocked unconscious or worse. They broke contact and circled again.

"Yes; I was right; you are good but now we both know that I'm better." Natalie smiled.

"The only thing you're better at is flapping your gums. If this was a talking contest I'd be dead already."

Although she would never admit it, Natalie bridled at Becky's retort and launched a ferocious combination of blows that Becky barely blocked or dodged. Under the flurry of blows Becky could do nothing but retreat, as she did so her foot hit a large fallen branch and she was momentarily distracted; she looked away.

This was all the opening Natalie needed, her left fist hit Becky in the stomach and her right just missed the nerve cluster in Becky's temple as she fell to her knees, blood trickling from her mouth. Natalie took a step back.

She's done for. Blood from the mouth denotes internal bleeding. She'll be unconscious in a few seconds.

Almost on queue Becky reeled backwards and fell heavily on her back, both hands clutching at her abdomen. More blood spurted from her mouth, her breathing became rasp-like and her eyelids fluttered.

Shit! I didn't think I'd hit her hard enough to cause this much damage.

Natalie knelt by Becky and put both hands on her cheeks, twisting her head slowly to the side so she wouldn't choke on her own blood.

●●●

Wraith pushed the buttons on the security pad and the grey steel door clicked open. It was 5.33am and he had been waiting patiently in the shadows since before midnight to ensure the area was free of guards or police surveillance. He'd been on a previous mission and had to abort through a police presence. If Wraith had been the enemy they would have paid with their lives for such sloppy surveillance drills. Almost on cue Rocky had arrived to spend what was left of the night with his young mistress and Wraith watched as the apartment lights were extinguished twenty minutes later. Immediately before him were narrow steps in an ill-lit hall leading upstairs to the first floor landing. Wraith found a pressure pad under the carpet of the third step, if he hadn't found any security devices he would have been very disappointed as he believed he knew how his mark thought. At the penultimate step Wraith found another pressure pad.

One is none and two is one. I think I've heard that somewhere before.

Wraith smirked to himself as he made it to the landing. The only items of furniture and decoration were a hat stand, with Rocky's overcoat and a much smaller beige raincoat and a large original painting by a modern artist called Robert Heindel who specialised in painting dancers. This large framed painting depicted a male and female dancer mid-leap, Wraith liked it.

Wait a minute, something's not right here. Firstly that's a very expensive painting to have on the landing of a small apartment and secondly Rocky wasn't wearing an overcoat when he arrived here. Remember the training. If something doesn't look right, it probably isn't.

Wraith was even more cautious as he approached the only door on the landing. He'd studied both the picture and the hat stand and could find nothing to indicate any surveillance or security devices.

The lock on the door seems a pretty standard five-latch-lever. Why have the pressure pads then a flimsy lock on the door? It doesn't make sense.

"If I see you even breath heavily, I'll gun you down where you stand," came the steady female voice from behind him. A sharp jab in his back with the muzzle punctuated the words. "Raise your hands very slowly. If you move them too fast you'll never move them again."

Shit! Where did she come from?

Wraith raised his hands carefully. He could recognise the control with which the commands were given, this wasn't your everyday thug. She was definitely a serious player.